FREE LANCE AND THE FIELD OF BLOOD

PAUL STEWART is the author of many books for children including *The Wakening*. In recent years he has collaborated extensively with illustrator Chris Riddell, most notably on the hugely successful series *The Edge Chronicles*, *The Blobheads* series and *Muddle Earth*. He lives in Brighton with his wife and two children.

CHRIS RIDDELL is the acclaimed cartoonist for *The Observer* newspaper and the highly successful illustrator of a wide variety of books for children including Kate Greenaway Medal winner *Pirate Diary*. He also lives in Brighton with his wife and three children.

FREE LANCE AND THE FIELD OF BLOOD

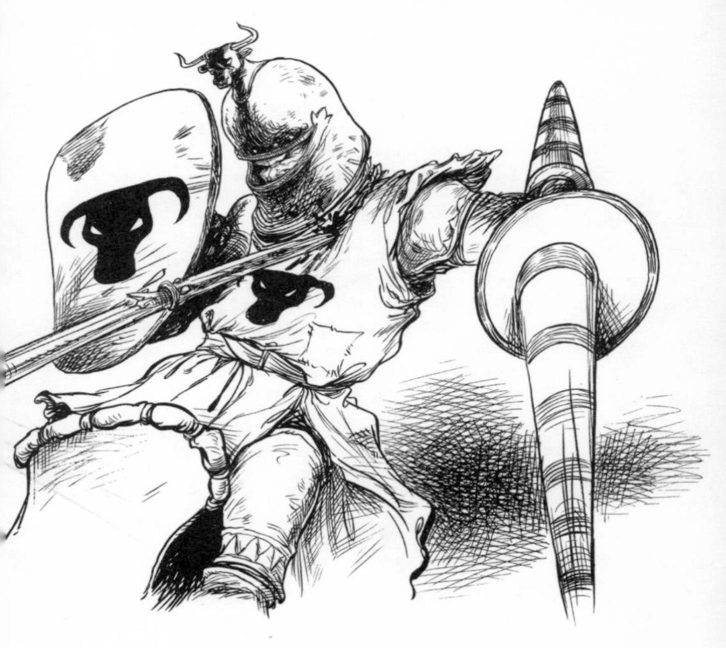

a division of Hodder Headline Limited

For Anna and Jack

Published in Great Britain in 2004
by Hodder Children's Books.

10 9 8 7 6 5 4 3 2 1

Consultant: Wendy Cooling

A Catalogue record for this book is available from the British Library.

ISBN 0 340 874066

Printed and bound by Clays Ltd, St Ives plc

The paper used in this book is a natural recyclable product made from wood grown in sustainable forests. The hardcover board is recycled.

Hodder Children's Bo
A division of Hodder Headline Limited
338 Euston Road, London

1

'I'm making you an offer, sir knight,' said the duke, standing up to leave. 'An offer you can't refuse.'

'No,' I said quietly. 'I don't suppose I can.'

As he left, I slumped back in my chair. *He* was a powerful duke, *I* was a mere free lance. What choice did I have?

*

And to think, it had all looked so promising three days earlier. After a late start and a leisurely ride, it was late afternoon when the castle of the duke of the Western Marches came into view. With a twitch of the reins, I steered Jed across a broad river and up the bank on the far side. As the tournament field opened up before us, Jed pawed the ground.

'Easy, boy,' I said.

I knew how he felt. Jed was a thoroughbred Arbuthnot grey. Jousting was in his blood, and it had been a long time since we'd seen a scene as magnificent as this.

'Welcome home, Jed,' I whispered.

The tournament field was ablaze with colour. There were penants and banners; tents and marquees. The air was charged with loud voices and a tangy, mouth-watering mixture of smells: leather, manure and a hog turning on a spit.

Yes, it felt good to be back at a major castle tournament.

I checked out the opposition. All the usual types were there. A boastful-looking customer – all swagger and confidence, and a snarling boar's head crest. A rich young nobleman with a fine tent, four squires and a pack of white hounds – out for some excitement on the tournament field, while daddy picked up the bill. And to my left, standing beside a particularly flashy marquee, a showman knight.

I had to laugh. With his baubles and tat, he was nothing if not eye-catching. Yet, judging by the tournament victories embroidered on his silk pennant, he certainly knew how to handle a lance.

Further along, I came to a cluster of more modest tents belonging to the knights from the Farmlands of the East. Big, stout petty-nobles, they were. Some were quite handy with a lance, it's true – but to be honest, they were all far better-suited to driving a plough.

Rich or poor, all the knights present had one thing on their minds. The prize money. The winner of the tournament would take away a purse of fifty gold pieces.

Fifty gold pieces! That was more than you could win in a whole year of manor-house tournaments.

The place was packed. Apart from the knights, there were smithies and armourers, merchants and servants, valets and squires –

and, no doubt, the pickpockets and other ne'er-do-wells who never fail to appear at such gatherings, where the ale flows freely and the pickings are rich.

Close to the outer castle walls were the stables, where grooms tended to the masters' horses.

One – a powerfully built black war horse – caught my eye, and I wondered who might own such a fine-looking beast.

Probably the Rich Kid, I thought, and patted Jed on the neck. 'Looks like you've got competition too,' I said.

'You there!' cried a high-pitched voice. 'Where do you think you're going?'

I turned to see a fussy looking individual glaring back at me. He had red leggings, lace cuffs and collar, a tabard like a duchess's table cloth – and a seriously bad haircut. Think of a fat black pudding boiled in goose fat and you'll get the idea.

'Are you talking to me?' I asked casually.

'I most certainly am,' he squeaked, and flapped a piece of parchment at me. 'Are you on the list? Have you wegistered?'

'Registered?' I said.

'I am the hewald,' he said.

'Herald,' I said.

'If you wish to participate in the jousting tournament, you must wegister with me. Dismount and pwesent yourself.'

I'd seen his type before. Fussy little men who enjoyed ordering others around.

'I am a free lance,' I told him, 'up from the Manor-House Circuit.'

The herald's top lip curled. 'I'm afwaid you'll find a Castle Tournament much more taxing,' he said. 'You'll be up against the finest knights in the land.' He looked me up and down. 'I mean, are you quite sure you're good enough?'

Without saying a word, I reached inside my saddle-bag. I was good enough all right. I'd won my last five tournaments, giving me the right to mix it with the big boys – and here were the certificates to prove it.

'I think you'll find everything's in order,' I said.

'Yes, yes,' he said, thrusting the papers back at me. He pulled a piece of charcoal from behind his ear and entered my name at the bottom of his list.

Free Lance.

I tried to hide my grin from old pudding head, but it was no good. After all those years of village greens and rundown manor houses, I was back at the Majors at last.

'Pitch your tent over there,' said the herald, flapping a hand toward a thistle-strewn patch of grass beside the stable enclosure. It was far from ideal, but at least I'd be close to Jed. 'The tournament starts at midday,' he said, turning away and striding off.

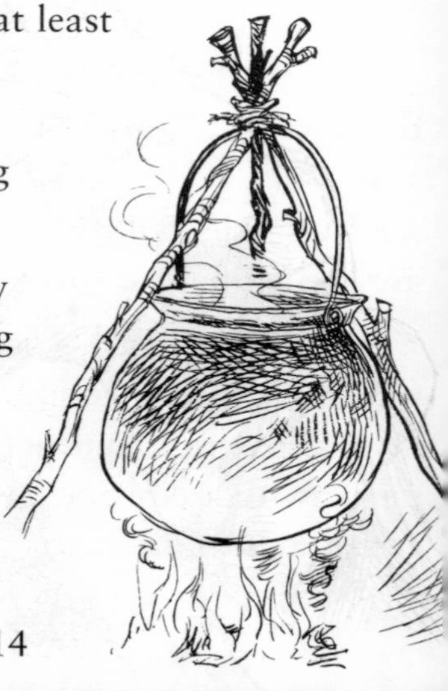

I lit a fire, pitched my tent and was soon sitting down to a supper of 'Squire's Stew' – rabbit, snared at sunrise and stewed at sunset, with field mushrooms and wild herbs thrown in for good measure. This is the life, I thought.

All round me, the bonded knights were being waited on hand and foot by their squires. Not that I was envious. Not for a moment. Along with the pampering came a lifetime of serving their master. I'd tried it once, and knew it wasn't for me.

I am a free lance. My own man.

'Are you hiring, sir?' came a squeaky voice.

I looked up to see a lanky, flaxen-haired youth with a big nose, a slack jaw and spots standing in front of me. His tattered jerkin was stained with the remains of his last meal – which, from the look of it, had been eaten at least two days earlier.

'I'm not sure I can afford a fine squire like yourself,' I said.

'I'm very cheap, sir,' said the youth. 'All I need is me keep – and a tenth share of any winnings, of course.'

He shrugged. 'I've tried all the others, sir, but most of them just laughed. But I'm a hard worker. I can polish your armour, groom your horse and fetch firewood. I'm very good at fetching firewood...'

Something told me I was going to regret this. But then, the kid looked as though he could do with a break.

'All right,' I said, 'you're hired, if...'

'If, sir?'

'If you don't mind Squire's Stew.'

'Oh, I love it, sir,' he squeaked.

I handed him a plate. 'What's your name, lad?'

'Wormrick,' he said.

'Then tuck in, Wormrick. We've got a busy day tomorrow.'

Just how busy, I found out soon enough. From the moment her ladyship's silver handerkerchief fluttered down from her snow-white fingers, Jed and I were at it non-stop.

A field-of-silver joust is a straight-forward affair. All you have to do is knock your opponent from the saddle. After a slow start Jed and I got into

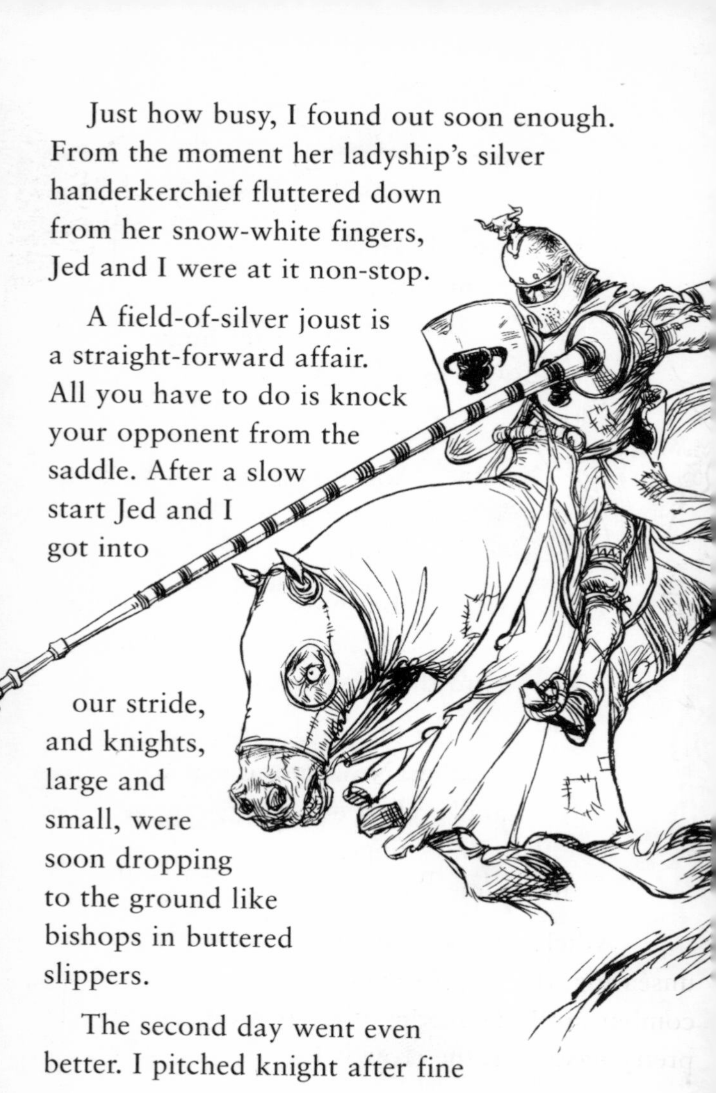

our stride, and knights, large and small, were soon dropping to the ground like bishops in buttered slippers.

The second day went even better. I pitched knight after fine

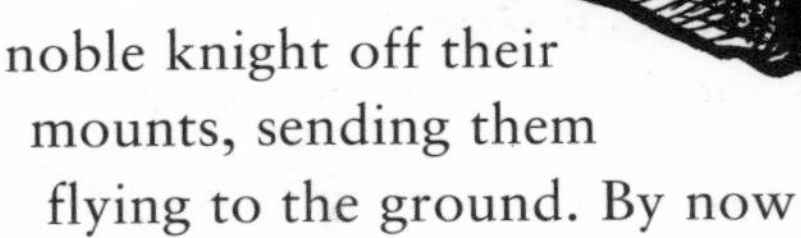

noble knight off their mounts, sending them flying to the ground. By now the crowd was getting excited. The bets were flying, and a lot of people were making a lot of money on yours truly.

But not me. *I* wouldn't see a brass penny unless I made it to the semi-finals.

On the third day, things got tougher. Now it was a gold handkerchief dropping from her ladyship's fingers that got the tournament underway.

A field-of-gold joust is one where, after the unseating, the knights engage in hand-to-hand combat until one or the other gives up. It can get pretty nasty, but the crowds love it.

I got the boastful customer with the snarling boar's head crest in the first round. He went down hard, breaking his leg in three places – and wasn't boasting any more.

Next up was the showman knight, and I knew I had trouble on my hands. I unseated him on our first charge, but he sprang back to his feet like a foxhound with its tail on fire. The crowd roared as he set about me with his broadsword.

I bided my time, taking what he was dishing out, because I knew his sort. Can't resist playing to the crowd and trying one clever move too many. Sure enough, it wasn't long before Showman danced past me with a disguised right hand slice – and I had him! A swift shield uppercut and a short, sharp body-blow, and the show was over.

Later, back in my tent, Wormrick fussed about my injuries. With a bit of luck, there was nothing that a bit of strapping wouldn't see to. I was through to the semi-finals and, as Wormrick finished with me and went off to see to Jed, I pictured the opponent who awaited me the next day.

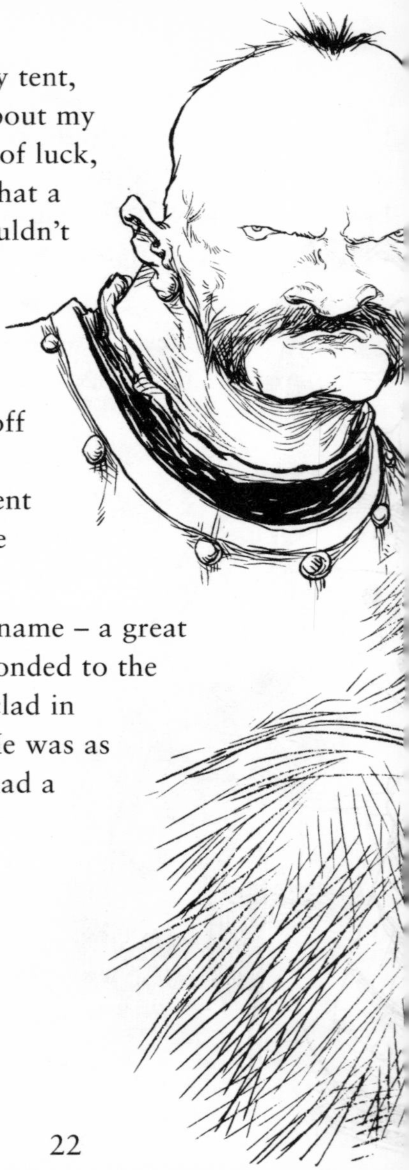

Hengist was his name – a great brute of a fellow, bonded to the castle, and always clad in dull grey armour. He was as hard as nails, and had a grim reputation for fighting dirty.

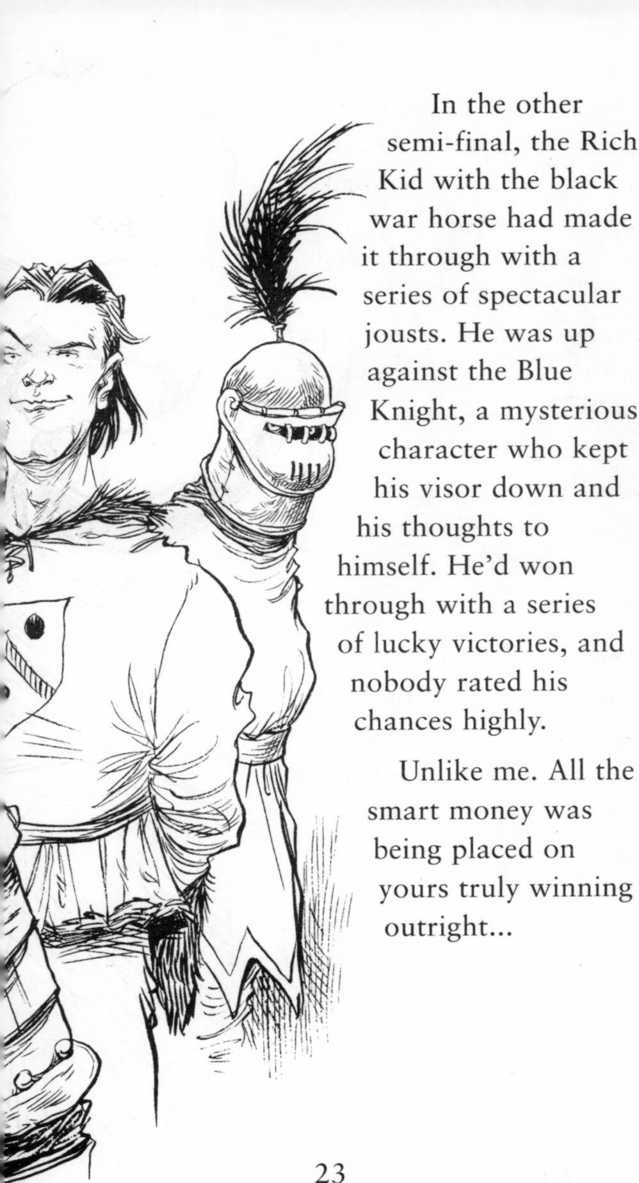

In the other semi-final, the Rich Kid with the black war horse had made it through with a series of spectacular jousts. He was up against the Blue Knight, a mysterious character who kept his visor down and his thoughts to himself. He'd won through with a series of lucky victories, and nobody rated his chances highly.

Unlike me. All the smart money was being placed on yours truly winning outright...

Just then, the tent flaps opened and in walked the duke of the Western Marches himself. I'd seen him watching the events from the royal throne – and noticed the glint in his eyes as he'd won bet after bet on me winning. Close up, he was fatter than I'd thought and, with his pointed yellow teeth and flapping ermine cloak, looked like nothing so much as an overfed wolfhound.

'You seem to be doing well,' he barked. 'People will make a lot of money if you defeat Hengist.'

I nodded, taking his words for a compliment. I should have known better.

'But you're not going to do that,' he said sharply.

'I'm not?' I said.

'No, you're going to lose,' he said. His jagged teeth glinted in the lamplight. 'But make sure you lose convincingly. No one must suspect a thing...'

'And why would I do this?' I asked.

An unpleasant smile spread out across Duke Wolfhound's fat face. 'There's a purse of thirty gold pieces for you now,' he said, 'and thirty more later, when you've taken a tumble.'

'And if I don't?' I said.

His yellow eyes narrowed. 'Then I shall be forced to tell the herald that your documents are forged. You'll be thrown out on your ear.' He sneered. 'And don't think I couldn't.'

I didn't doubt it for a moment.

'It's a good offer,' said the duke. 'An offer you can't refuse.'

'No,' I said. 'I don't suppose I can.

*

So there I was, slumped in my chair, my head spinning.

Duke Wolfhound wanted me to throw the joust! Me, Free Lance, throw a joust! I've never thrown a joust in my life!

Not that the offer wasn't tempting. I'd make more by *losing* the tournament than I would by *winning* it.

And as a free lance, that sort of money wasn't to be sniffed at. Then again, there was the matter of honour. Even if no one ever discovered what I had done, *I would know...*

Just then, the tent flaps opened a second time, and a tall, slim figure dressed in a long hooded cape stepped in.

'We must speak at once, sir knight,' came a voice – a *woman's* voice. 'It is a matter of the utmost urgency.'

2

Call me a fool, but I've always had a soft spot for a damsel in distress.

'How can I help?' I asked her.

'I... I hardly know where to begin,' she faltered.

'You could start by lowering your hood,' I suggested.

A snow-white hand emerged from a sleeve of her gown and pulled down the hood. A mass of auburn ringlets tumbled forward, and two dazzling emerald-green eyes fixed me in their tearful gaze.

It was her ladyship – the one who'd done the handkerchief dropping at the tournament. She looked as if she could do with a handkerchief now. I offered her mine, which she dabbed to her eyes, and then held out to me.

'Keep it,' I said. 'Now, what's this all about? Shouldn't you be up at the castle preparing for this evening's banquet.'

'Oh, sir knight,' she cried. 'You've got to help me! I beg you! You hold my future in your hands.'

'I do?' I said.

'I followed my uncle here,' she said. 'I knew he was up to no good, and when I heard...' Her face crumpled and the tears began streaming down her face once more.

'Calm yourself, your ladyship,' I said.

'I... I heard him make you an offer,' she sobbed. 'Promised you extra money if you threw the tournament. But you must not listen to him,' she said urgently.

'No?' I said.

'I know my uncle,' she said. 'He's set this whole thing up. And it's not the first time. He holds a tournament, waits for a champion like yourself to appear – a champion who can't lose, who everyone has placed their bets on. Then he places his money on the other knight – *his* man – and makes the champion an offer he can't refuse...'

'*His* man?' I said.

Her ladyship shuddered. 'Hengist,' she said, her voice laced with disgust. 'And what's more,' she whispered, 'if he *does* win... then... Oh,' she sobbed, 'my uncle has promised him my hand in marriage. It doesn't matter that Hengist is brutal and cruel, only that he is loyal – and that I should be the reward for that loyalty.'

'But what's this got to do with me?' I asked.

'Everything, brave sir knight!' she said.

I liked "brave". She'd really got my attention now.

'I have come here to beg you not to lose the joust tomorrow,' she said. 'If you defeat Hengist, and I know you can, then he will be disgraced in my uncle's eyes – and he will punish him by calling off our marriage.' She fluttered her eyelashes. 'And you will have saved a helpless maiden from a fate worse than death.'

I shrugged. 'What's to stop him marrying you off to another of his henchmen instead?' I asked.

'I won't allow that to happen,' said her ladyship defiantly. 'Even now, the one I love is planning our escape, an escape that will fail if Hengist gets his brutal hands on me tomorrow.

So you see, I need your help,' she said, '*valiant* sir knight, *courageous* sir knight...'

She was certainly pressing all the right buttons now, but I was in a pretty pickle, and knew it. If I threw the joust, then the beautiful girl would end up married to Hengist the Henchman. If I didn't, the duke himself would be after me. I'd find myself thrown out of the tournament faster than a steaming chamber-pot from a bedroom window.

Thing is, I'm a sucker for a pretty face, and they didn't come much prettier than her ladyship's.

'Don't worry,' I heard myself saying. 'Whatever happens tomorrow, I give you my word as a knight, that Hengist won't lay a finger on *you*.'

Her ladyship squeezed my hand. 'I knew I could count on you, dear, *sweet* knight.'

And with that, she turned and hurried away. I smiled after her stupidly, my promise ringing in my ears. What *was* I going to do tomorrow?

Just then, Wormrick's matted hair and spotty face appeared at the tent flap. 'The horses are all jittery, sir,' he said, his voice high-pitched and breathless. 'Something's spooked them.'

'Rats, perhaps,' I suggested. 'Or maybe a snake. I'd better take a look. The last thing I need is something happening to Jed, along with everything else.'

'Everything else?' said Wormrick.

'You don't want to know, Wormrick,' I said. 'Come. To the stables.'

The sound of troubled whinnying and neighing greeted us as

we approached the makeshift stabling enclosures. The horses had been spooked all right.

As we approached, a tall, raven-haired beauty emerged from the shadows. She stopped when she saw us.

'I'm looking for my mistress,' she said, fixing me with her dark eyes. 'The lady of the castle.'

'You won't find her in there,' said Wormrick. 'That's the stables.'

Her ladyship's maid shot him a poisonous look.

'Your mistress has returned to the castle,' I said. 'Now, if you'll excuse us, I have a horse to attend to.'

A flicker of a smile played on the maid's lips as she stepped back to let us pass.

In the stables, the tethered horses were all skittering around, stamping their hoofs and tossing their heads. The Rich Kid's black war horse had broken out of its stall and was rearing up, pawing the air with its front legs. Its eyes were rolling and glistening froth was dripping from the sides of its mouth.

I pushed past a squire – hopping about uselessly from one leg to the other – and approached the panic-stricken horse, arms wide and talking horsey sweet-nothings in a low, calm voice. The horse snorted and backed away, but I could tell by the way its ears twitched, that it was paying attention.

'Easy, now,' I murmured. 'Nobody's going to hurt you.'

Its eyes stopped rolling and, when I patted its neck, it turned and licked my hand. I've always had a way with horses. I only hoped Jed wasn't getting jealous.

The squire stepped forward. 'Thank you kindly, sir,' he said. 'All the horses have been terrible jumpy. Maybe the hay's gone sour...'

I looked round at the upturned drinking trough and splintered stall. 'Maybe,' I said. 'Still, they seem all right now.' I turned to the war horse. 'Eh boy?' I said.

The horse whinnied softly and blew warm air into my face.

'Hey, you,' came a snooty voice. 'What do you think you're doing with my horse?'

I turned, to find the Rich Kid standing before me, his hands on his hips. He was dressed in expensive-looking clothes, ready for the banquet no doubt. There was silver thread embroidered on his surcoat, and a ruby-encrusted gold buckle on his belt. The whole lot must have cost daddy a pretty packet!

Our eyes met.

'What *are* you?' he sneered. 'A squire? A *serf*?'

'He's a knight,' said Wormrick indignantly. 'And he just calmed your horse down. Why, the poor creature was in such a state it'd probably have broken its legs if he hadn't.'

'Knight, eh?' said the Rich Kid, looking me up and down. 'Sorry, old chap, didn't recognize you as a fellow knight. Still...' He eyed my patched tunic with evident distaste. 'You've got to admit, it's an easy mistake to make.'

I didn't rise to the bait – even though I sensed Wormrick would have enjoyed it if I had. The Rich Kid turned on his own squire.

'What have you to say for yourself, eh?'

'P... please, sir,' the terrified squire stammered. 'One minute he was fine, the next I couldn't do a thing with him, and...'

'I don't have time for all this now,' the Rich Kid interrupted. 'Some of us have banquets to go to.'

'Yes... S...sorry, sir,' said the squire.

'Rub him down and settle him in another stall,' he called back as he strode to the door. 'And if he gets troublesome again, take the whip to him.'

I snorted. 'Best way to ruin a good horse.'

The Rich Kid spun round. 'When I want your opinion, sir knight, I'll ask for it,' he snapped. 'Free lances,' he muttered as he strode out. 'Scum of the tournaments.'

He was certainly pushing his luck, and under different circumstances, I'd have taught him a lesson he wouldn't forget. But this was neither the time nor the place. Sometimes, in my line of work, a thick skin serves you far better than a quick temper. There would be time enough to teach him better manners on the jousting field.

I crossed the stable to where Jed was tethered. He seemed fine. I patted him, nuzzled my face against his, and told him he was the finest horse a knight could wish for. Wormrick came up behind me.

'When you've quite finished,' he laughed, 'Jed needs his supper. And *you've* got a banquet to go to, remember.'

'You're right, Wormrick,' I said. I pulled some bits of straw from my hair, brushed myself down and turned to face him. 'How do I look?' I asked.

Wormrick grinned. 'Not bad for a free lance,' he said.

That was good enough for me. 'See that Jed is fed and watered, and help yourself to supper in the tent,' I told him as I set off for the banquet.

'And get a good night's sleep.'

'I will, Sir,' squeaked Wormrick.

It was quite an honour to dine inside the castle itself, and I *had* made it to the semi-finals – yet I felt none of the excitement and pride I'd expected to feel. Instead, as I clattered over the drawbridge, I couldn't get the sight of her ladyship's pleading emerald-green eyes out of my head, nor the sound of the duke's voice making me an offer I couldn't refuse.

3

I seized the heavy handles of the banqueting hall doors, and pushed them open. As I stepped inside, a blast of heat, noise and smells struck me like a hammer blow.

The hall was tall and grand, with ivy-decorated pillars, flags fluttering from the high vaulted ceiling and fresh straw upon the floor. To my right, a great fire was roaring.

I was late, that much was clear. All round me, the banquet was in full swing, with the knights and squires at the long trestle tables shouting loudly as they tucked into their bread and stew and supped their penny ale.

There were musicians in the gallery playing jolly reels. There were jugglers and tumblers and a character on stilts, all performing on the straw-covered floor – and taking care not to step on the huge, grey-haired hounds that lounged about, gnawing on the mutton bones tossed to them by their masters.

Noisiest of all, was the jester, a tiny fellow with bells on his hat and a voice, more shrill than a princess caught on the privy. Leaping about astride a hobby horse, a rough wooden sword in his hand, he was in the middle of some kind of mock-battle with a snappy terrier dressed like a dragon...

'Your name, sir?' came a voice, shouting above the din. I turned to see a page with a roll of parchment in his hands looking me up and down sniffily.

'I'm probably on your list as Free Lance,' I replied.

For a moment the page scanned the parchment. When he spotted my name, his eyebrows shot upwards.

'Oh, yes, indeed, sir,' he said. 'Follow me, sir.'

I went with him, between the rows of knights and squires towards the high table at the far end of the hall. Some of them turned from their bread and stew and raised their tankards to me; others cheered.

'Fine jousting, sir knight!' someone cried, and the cheering grew rowdier.

I acknowledged their praise with a modest nod of my head, and noticed Duke Wolfhound eyeing me suspiciously. As the page led me up onto a low platform, I found myself standing before him. I bowed low, as ceremony demanded.

Duke Wolfhound – face flushed and fangs glinting – raised his goblet to me. 'Eat, drink and make merry, sir knight,'

he said. 'You have an important day tomorrow.'

I nodded. 'Thank you, sir,' I said. 'Indeed I have.'

The duke threw back his head and roared with laughter, as if I had just told him the most hilarious joke. To his left, Hengist – a huge leg of dripping lamb in his hand – leaned across and whispered something into the duke's ear which made him laugh all the louder.

The page ushered me on towards my seat. As I passed her ladyship, seated to the duke's left, she stared at me, her emerald eyes welling with tears.

Don't forget, she mouthed silently.

Forget? There was no chance of me forgetting what she'd told me. Not forgetting was easy. Deciding what to do about it was proving much more difficult.

I took my place. To my right was a matronly woman in dowdy clothes; beyond her, the Rich Kid. He was waving away a platter of meat like the spoilt brat that he was, and demanding a flagon of their finest wine. I turned away in disgust. To my left was an empty seat.

'Who's meant to be sitting there?' I asked a page, as he filled my tankard with thick twopenny ale.

'The Blue Knight, sir,' he replied. 'But he's been keeping himself to himself all tournament.'

I nodded. Given his dismal jousting skills, I wasn't surprised that he'd hit on the gimmick of being mysterious to keep the crowds interested. He'd had some really lucky victories – opponents' horses bolting or throwing their riders. Then again, you get those in any tournament, and fluke or no fluke, he *had* ended up in the semi-finals.

'What would sir care to start with?' came a voice, as a second page appeared at my shoulder.

There was salmon and trout, patés and truffles, and quivering moulds of larks' tongues in aspic...

'I think I'll try a little bit of everything,' I said.

The two pages leaped into action. I tucked in. Everything tasted even better than it looked – apart from the jellied larks' tongues, which I threw to the dogs.

The second course was even more spectacular; suckling pigs with apples in their mouths, roasted peacocks dressed in their own feathers, capons and pheasants, and silver platters of sliced meats, dripping with sauces. The pages saw to my every need, slicing and serving, and never allowing my tankard get less than half full.

I would have preferred to eat in silence, but the matron to my right – aunt of the duke, as I soon discovered – was having none of it. She talked of the weather, of the seasons, of her relatives, of prayer and duty, of the freshness of the straw and the brightness of the candles – not to mention the second-rate jester.

'His performance is *so* boring,' she yawned. 'We've seen this George and the Dragon business so many times before.'

I nodded, but made no reply. She didn't seem to notice, but kept on talking – her theme now the colours of the flags hanging above our heads, and how red did so clash with green.

I looked round. The Rich Kid was tossing lumps of meat to his white hounds. Hengist and Duke Wolfhound were deep in conversation.

Her ladyship sat staring straight ahead of her, not touching the food laid before her by her raven-haired handmaid. When two of the white wolfhounds got into a vicious fight over a scrap of meat, the handmaid looked over at the Rich Kid as he struggled to part them, a look of unpleasant amusement on her face.

'Ah, now this is more like it,' said the matron, nudging me in the ribs. 'The troubadour.'

I looked round, to see a tall young fellow, dressed in simple clothes, striding to the front of the minstrel-gallery and strumming his lute. The revellers fell still. The troubadour burst into song.

'*My Lords and Ladies, listen well,*' he sang, his voice – like all troubadours so far as I am concerned – far too high-pitched, like a knight in tight leggings. He made his way down the stairs. '*I have a chivalrous tale to tell...*'

Beside me, the matron sighed longingly and closed her eyes. The knights on the low tables seemed equally spellbound. For my part, I'd heard it all before – endless tales of sweet damsels and wicked villains, and a knight in shining armour who arrives to put everything right.

Life just wasn't that simple. And I should know – even though there were some who believed that it was, I thought, turning to look at her ladyship.

Her expression took me by surprise. She was looking up, her unblinking gaze staring at the troubadour as he crossed the hall. Her face was radiant – her lips softly parted and eyes gleaming with excitement.

'So *that's* her loved one!' I groaned. If she was in love with a troubadour, then she was in more trouble than I thought.

I continued my meal, deep in thought. Her ladyship had been promised to a great hulking knight, and with only a troubadour to turn to for help! No wonder she needed *my* help. Certainly, the troubadour didn't look as if he'd be much use if it came to any rough stuff, and he probably didn't have two brass farthings to call his own. My heart went out to the young lovers.

Life could be complicated and difficult all right.

The song finished and Duke Wolfhound climbed noisily to his feet, a brimming goblet raised high.

'Sir knights, one and all!' he bellowed. 'A toast to our semi-finalists! May the best man win!'

'May the best man win!' the crowd roared ›ack.

Beside me, the matron tapped me on the arm. I have so enjoyed our little chat,' she said. Good luck, tomorrow, sir knight.'

I acknowledged her words with a smile and a ıod. But I knew that the only luck I'd have was vhat old Wolfhound allowed me.

4

As the sun reached its highest point in the sky, Jed and I made our way across the tournament field. I could tell by the way he tossed his head and pawed the ground that he was impatient to get underway. As for me, it was another story. I felt lousy! My limbs were heavy, my chest ached, and my head felt as if it had been stuffed with goose down.

The trouble was, I was exhausted. I hadn't slept a wink all night. I just couldn't stop thinking about the fix I was in.

Should I throw the joust, as Duke Wolfhound wanted, and walk away with a heavy purse? Or should I fight fair and save her ladyship, but risk a heavy beating from Wolfhound's thugs? My head said one thing, my heart said another, and I lay awake all night trying to choose. The early-morning light was streaming in through the holes of my moth-eaten tent before I decided at last what to do.

I wasn't proud of my decision, I can tell you. It went against every knightly fibre of my body. But though I hated to do it, there was nothing else for it. I would go down to Hengist.

Of course, I'd make it look good. I'd flip from Jed's back and, taking care to cushion my fall, land on the ground in a clatter of armour and a cloud of dust – but then stay down...

Afterwards, I'd collect my promised gold from Duke Wolfhound and tell him to let her ladyship go, or I'd shop him to the herald and bring his tournament-rigging days to an end.

And if Hengist had a problem with that, we could have a nice little chat about it, away from the tournament field. I also decided that I'd give her ladyship half the gold so that she and the troubadour could travel far away and live happily ever after.

As plans went, it wasn't great; the herald might side with the duke, Hengist might prove to be a bit of handful, and her ladyship might end up at the top of a tall tower with no staircase. But in the circumstances, it was the best I could come up with.

Just then, a trumpet sounded loudly and I looked round to see the herald waddling to the centre of the field. The first joust was about to begin.

'At the south end, in wed and white stwipes,' the herald proclaimed, 'I give you bwave Sir Walph of Mountjoy!'

The crowd cheered.

'At the north end,' the herald continued. 'Dwessed in blue, the... errm... the Blue Knight!'

The cheers grew louder. Everyone loves an underdog.

The herald raised his arms. The crowd fell silent. All eyes turned towards her ladyship, who rose to her feet and let a glittering handkerchief flutter down over the balcony. It landed on the grass.

The herald inspected it. 'Let the field-of-gold joust commence!' he cried.

At the second trumpet blast, the Rich Kid spurred his black war horse viciously. The animal sprang forward, its ears flat back, its muzzle foaming, the whites of its eyes glinting wildly as it tossed its head. It looked like a creature possessed.

Glancing over at the Duke, I noticed the raven-haired handmaid standing behind her ladyship, her dark, glaring eyes fixed on the horse and rider.

At the other end of the field, I saw the Blue Knight urging his bony-looking nag forward. I shook my head. Whoever the Blue Knight was, he certainly wasn't a natural jouster. He rode like an east-country bumpkin, and couldn't hold his lance steady if his life depended on it – and the way it was looking, it just might, because the Rich Kid had got into his stride now.

Keeping the war horse on target with a tight rein, he levelled his lance and brought his opponent into his sights. It was a lovely move, one even *I* would have been proud to perform. The Blue Knight didn't stand a chance.

At least, that was what I thought. But at that moment, an extraordinary thing happened. Just as the two knights were about to clash, the black war horse let out a terrible whinnying screech, arched its back and crashed headlong into the tournament turf, pitching the Rich Kid high up in the air – and onto the Blue Knight's wavering lance.

There was a bone-shattering crunch, the splintering of wood, and a turf-shuddering crash as the Rich Kid hit the ground. He didn't move. The herald strode across the field and poked the crumpled body with his toe.

'Victowy!' he cried and raised his arm. 'The Blue Knight will go through to the final.'

The crowd seemed confused. Only a couple of half-hearted cheers rose above the gathering murmur. No one could quite believe what they'd seen. For a healthy war horse simply to collapse like that was unheard of.

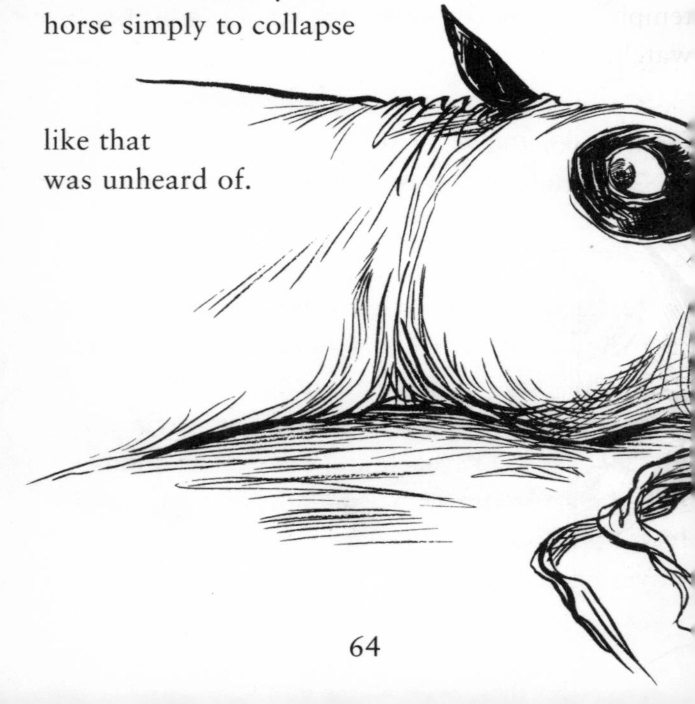

The Rich Kid's four squires rushed forwards and fussed about their master. I was more concerned about the stricken war horse. Dismounting, I strode over and knelt down beside it. The poor creature whimpered, one wild eye staring back at me. There was blood at its mouth, and its front legs were broken.

'There, there, boy,' I said. There was nothing I could do.

I looked up to see a man-at-arms approaching with a crossbow. I knew that a bolt through the temple was the kindest thing, but I still couldn't watch. I turned away.

'Come, come, sir knight, it is time,' came a familiar voice, and I felt old pudding-head tugging at my arm.

'Sad of course that the horse must be put down,' he said, 'but these things happen.'

I nodded. He was right of course. As he led me away, I noticed the raven-haired handmaid, her eyes boring into mine. I looked away, shocked by the thin smile playing on her lips.

'Huwwy up,' said the herald impatiently. 'The joust must commence without further delay.'

I climbed back onto Jed's back and took my place at the south end of the tournament field.

We waited as the war horse was dragged off, and the Rich Kid – moaning softly now – was stretchered away by his four squires. A ripple of anticipation ran through the crowd. I nodded to those who were cheering me on and raised my head proudly. I might as well enjoy those cheers while they lasted.

I, a free lance, had made it to the semi-finals of a major castle tournament. It was only a shame that, on the second tilt, I would have to go down as hard as the Rich Kid before me – and the cheers would turn to boos when the crowd realized that the favourite they'd bet so much on was not getting up.

At the other end of the field, Hengist had mounted his stallion. Clad in his dull grey armour, he cut an impressive figure – but was too slow and plodding to be a great jouster. At least, that was what I hoped.

As the trumpet sounded, the herald stepped forward. 'At the north end, we have Sir Hengist of the Western Marches.'

There were boos amid the cheers as the crowd greeted the local boy.

'At the south end,' the herald continued, 'Sir... um... Fwee Lance.'

For a second time that afternoon all eyes fell on her ladyship, who climbed to her feet and held the handkerchief high. As our eyes met, a smile fluttered uncertainly across her face. I lowered my visor.

The handkerchief fell.

'Let the field-of-gold joust commence!' cried the herald.

With a loud snort, Hengist spurred his horse. I twitched Jed's reins, and he was off. Beneath me, I could feel his pounding hoofs gathering speed. How he loved the tournaments; the charged air in his nostrils, the boiling blood coursing through his body.

I raised my shield, fixed my sights on Hengist, and levelled my lance. All brawn and no brain, the great oaf was lumbering towards me,

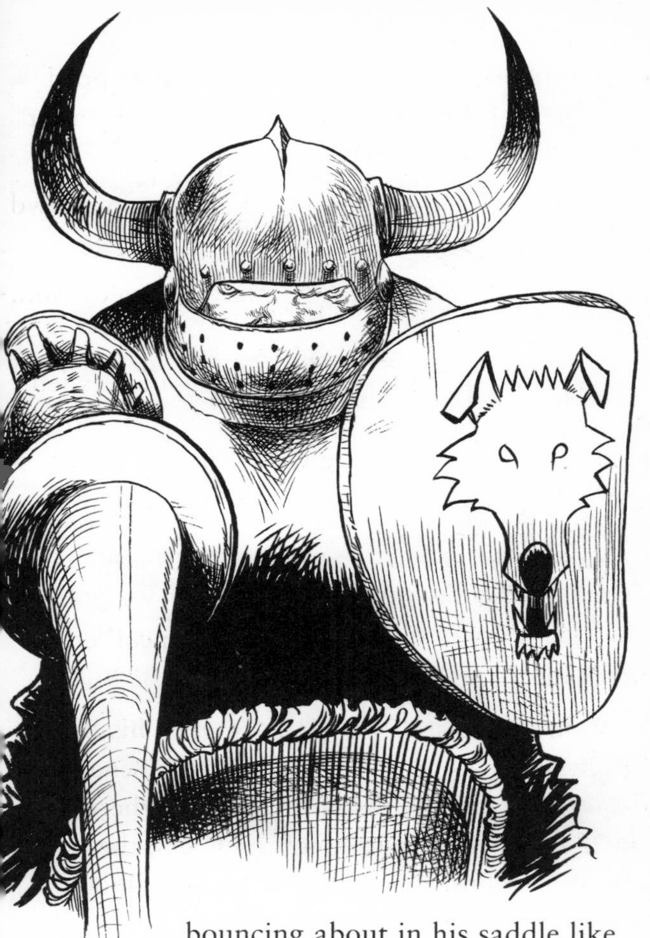

bouncing about in his saddle like
ın ale-barrow in an ox-cart. His great heavy
ırmour was doing him no favours either,
ɪitching him this way and that.

At a lance-length away, I saw he was leaning so heavily forward that he'd left himself wide open at the neck. I could have finished him off there and then. Instead, I turned my lance away, and took a glancing blow to my shield as Hengist thundered past.

The crowd gave a loud gasp of surprise.

On the second joust, as we approached one another, I deliberately dropped my shoulder and raised my shield, offering a target that even a hopeless jouster like Hengist couldn't miss. Urging Jed on, I shifted my lance round so that it would glance harmlessly off his armour. Then, at the last possible moment, I slipped my feet from the stirrups and got ready for the heavy blow that I knew was about to come.

I wasn't disappointed. The air abruptly filled with the sound of shattering wood and a desperate cry from the crowd as Hengist's lance struck the top of my breastplate, and I shot from the saddle like a speared moat-fish.

I hit the ground hard, and rolled over and over, clattering like a brewer's barrel on cobblestones. If I had to go down, the least I could do was put on a show. I came to rest just near the grandstand – a nice touch, I thought – and lay there, stock still.

It was all over.

Through my visor, I glimpsed the shocked face of her ladyship looking down at me miserably, the colour drained from her cheeks. Beside her, Duke Wolfhound was smiling unpleasantly. He knew he'd won.

Just then, I became aware of a fierce stabbing pain in my shoulder where Hengist's lance had struck. I'd felt the blow of a blunted tournament lance many times before; a dull

bruising ache. But this was different. I put my hand to my shoulder and was shocked to feel the end of a shattered lance shaft.

I pulled myself up – to the gasps and cries of the crowd who had already written me off – and tugged at the length of splintered wood. I found myself holding the pointed iron tip of a war lance.

I'd been taken for a fool! A total sap! The duke had never intended to pay me for throwing the joust at all. He'd merely wanted me off my guard so that that great hulking henchman of his could finish me off for good. If I hadn't ridden the blow so well, I'd be dead now.

A red mist descended. I was gripped by a murderous rage.

I jumped to my feet, and as I drew my sword, the crowd gave a thunderous roar.

Hengist was lumbering towards me, his own broadsword gripped in a great ham of a hand. I threw myself at him, meeting his lunging uppercut with a high parry.

Our swords clashed, and I felt as if a red hot poker was boring into my shoulder. With a roar of pain, I dummied a high sword cut to his right, but swung low instead. It was an old trick, but one that caught Hengist totally off guard. As my broadsword sliced into the back of his knees, he crashed to the ground, bellowing like a wounded bear.

I stood over him, my sword raised high, about to bring it crashing down, when I felt a hand on my shoulder. It was the herald.

'There seems to have been a slight mix up with the lances,' he said out of the corner of his mouth, while smiling for the benefit of the cheering crowd. 'Most unfortunate, but we don't want it to get out of hand, do we?'

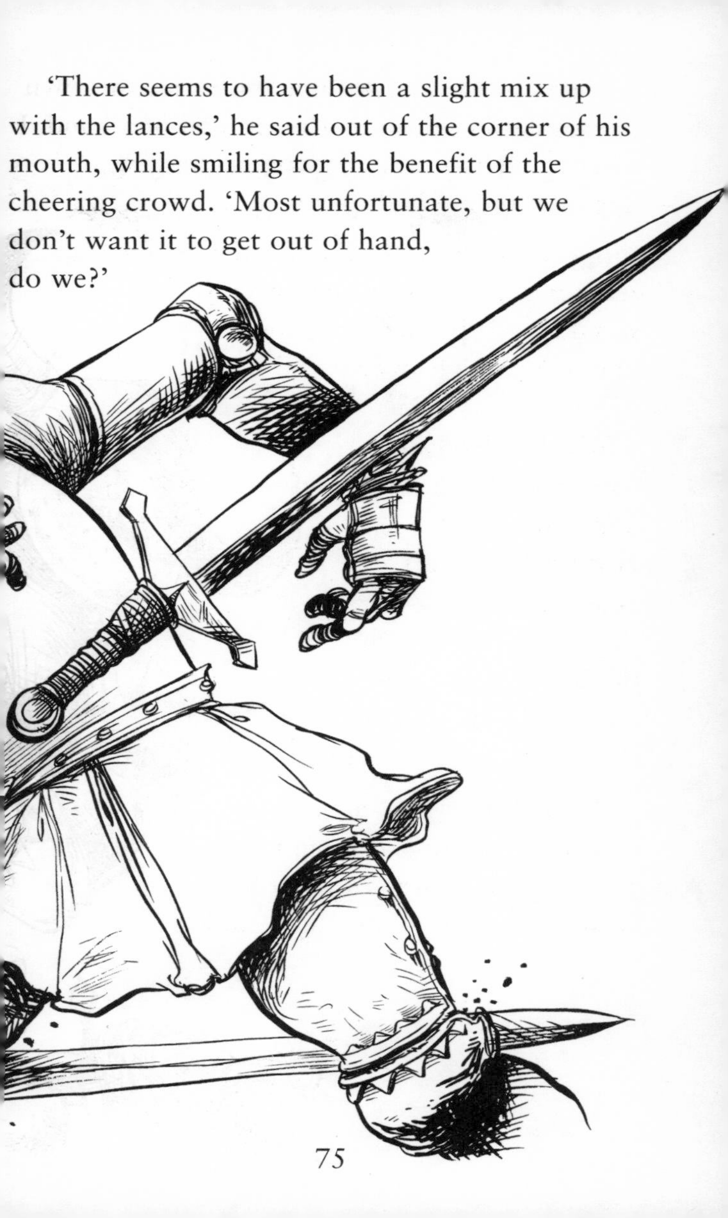

The red mist was lifting, and I suddenly felt very tired.

'After all,' the herald was saying, 'this is a field of gold, *not* a field of blood, wemember.'

I lowered my sword. My head was swimming and my shoulder hurt more than ever.

'My lords, ladies and gentlemen,' the herald announced loudly, 'Fwee Lance is through to the final!'

5

Her ladyship was staring down at me, her eyes brimming with tears of happiness and thanks. Beside her, Duke Wolfhound's face told a different story. With his eyes blazing and his fangs bared, he looked like a cornered dog in a bear pit.

He clicked his fingers and two beefy henchmen appeared at his side. At his whispered command, they clattered down the grandstand steps and lumbered onto the tournament field, their broadswords drawn.

Things were not looking good.

Then something surprising happened. As the

two goons approached, I heard a rising swell of noise behind me and turned to see a crowd of joyful spectators burst through the rope fence. Jostling Duke Wolfhound's goons aside, they seized me, hoisted me up onto their shoulders and carried me off, chanting my name loudly as they went.

'Free Lance! Free Lance!'

It was little wonder I was so popular, I realized, for most of the crowd had bet on me and were celebrating collecting their winnings. Everyone was laughing and cheering and clapping me on the back. Everyone, that is, except Duke Wolfhound.

From my vantage point, I could see him scowling at me. With a wave of his hand, he called off his henchmen. There was nothing any of them could do. At least, not for now.

But I knew the matter wouldn't stop there. Duke Wolfhound wasn't the sort to forgive and forget. The cold, calculating look on his face told me it wasn't his pride that was hurting him – it was his purse.

The crowd carried me round the tournament field three times, before trooping back to my tent. Wormrick came across to greet me.

'Well done, sir!' he said. 'I knew you could...' He gasped. 'Sir!' he exclaimed. 'You're bleeding!'

In all the excitement, I'd clean forgotten about my injury. Suddenly it all came flooding back. The lance blow. The pain. The blood... I looked down at my breast plate. It was dripping with the stuff.

I'm not usually the squeamish type. I've seen my fair share of brave knights cut down on the battlefield, but this was different. This was *my* blood – and lots of it! Wormrick's face swam before my eyes and my head suddenly felt heavier than a lead weight.

A black sea opened up before me – and I dived straight in.

*

I opened my eyes and tried to focus them. Slowly, the blurred shapes in front of me sharpened into a smiling mouth and two emerald-green eyes.

'You're awake,' her ladyship said, her voice breaking with relief. 'Thank goodness. I was beginning to fear the worst.'

'Your ladyship,' I said, sitting up, and immediately wishing I hadn't. A burning pain bored through my shoulder like a newly-forged nail.

'Easy now,' she said. 'Lie back again, sweet sir knight. Let me finish dressing your wound.'

I did as I was told, and sank back into the downy pillows and soft mattress. It was like floating on a cloud.

'Where am I?' I asked.

'The servants' quarters in the castle,' she said as she applied a thick, green ointment to my shoulder. The effect was so great, I almost expected to hear the hiss of steam as the wound cooled. 'I had you brought here because it wasn't safe for you to return to your tent. My uncle's henchmen are looking for you.'

I nodded grimly.

'But you have done me a great service, sir knight,' she continued, 'and I want to do everything I can to ensure you come to no harm.' She was bandaging me up as she spoke. 'Thankfully, your injuries are not too bad, but you must rest.'

'Rest!' I exclaimed. 'But the tournament... The *final*!'

'That's not till tomorrow,' said her ladyship firmly. 'So be a good knight, lie back, and let the ointment take effect. Besides,' she added, 'there are others far worse off than you.' A smile plucked at the corners of her mouth. 'Sir Hengist for one,' she said. 'My uncle's washed his hands of him and sent him packing.'

'So the wedding's off,' I said, smiling. 'Good job I didn't splash out on a wedding present.'

'You've done more than enough for me already,' she replied, returning my smile as she knotted the ends of the bandage underneath my arm. 'Thanks to you, my plans are complete. Tomorrow, when the tournament is over, I shall leave my uncle's castle for ever.'

'I wish you luck, your ladyship,' I said. 'It can be a harsh world beyond a castle's walls.'

'Luck has nothing to do with it,' she said, her green eyes gleaming with excitement. 'My beloved has arranged everything. He has two fine, strong horses waiting, and has bribed the castle gate-keeper with his last two gold crowns. It might be a harsh world as you say, but with him at my side I can face anything.' She smiled and planted a kiss on my forehead. 'And it's all thanks to you, sweet sir knight.'

'Don't mention it,' I said, lying back against the soft pillows, the touch of her lips lingering on my forehead.

Her ladyship straightened the blankets. 'All done,' she announced. 'Now, I must go and prepare myself for this evening's banquet. It wouldn't do to turn up late. My uncle mustn't suspect a thing.' She squeezed my hand warmly. 'Rest here, sir knight, until you're feeling completely recovered.'

With that, she turned and skipped from the room, seemingly without a care in the world. I hoped it would all work out for her. I'd done all I could. Now it was up to that troubadour of hers. I could only pray, for both their sakes, that he was up to the task. I had more than enough cares of my own right now.

Despite her ladyship's parting words, I could not risk remaining in bed a moment longer – however comfortable it might be. When the duke's henchmen found my tent empty, I knew they would try to get to me through Jed or Wormrick. I had to get back to them, and make sure they were all right.

Slipping reluctantly from beneath the warm bedcover, I shivered in my patched leggings and bare feet, and looked round the room for the rest of my clothes. I only hoped her ladyship hadn't sent them to the castle laundry.

At the end of the room stood a three-panelled wooden screen, behind which I could see the edge of a mirror and the corner of a chair sticking out. With a bit of luck, I'd find my missing clothes there as well.

I padded across the floor and looked. And there they were, all folded up neatly on the chair. It was the first bit of good luck I'd had all day. I quickly slipped the jerkin over my head, secured the sword around my waist and had just sat down to pull on my boots when I heard someone entering the room.

I froze. Had one of the duke's henchmen found me after all?

Gripping my sword, I leaned slowly forward in the chair and peered round the edge of the screen. There *was* someone in the room. But it was no guard. Instead, I found myself looking at her ladyship's raven-haired handmaid. She had something in her hand – a small phial or jar – and was unstoppering it as she made her way across the room.

The next moment, finding my bed empty, she stamped her foot petulantly and her eyes darted furiously around the room. There was something about her dark look that made me decide not to give myself away. I shrank back into the shadows behind the screen and waited.

The next moment there came a voice.

'So,' it said, 'looks like her ladyship's guest has flown the coop.' I edged myself forwards and peered through a hinged gap in the screen, to see the troubadour of all people striding into the room. 'And before you had a chance to weave your magic on him,' he said. 'How very unfortunate.'

The handmaid tossed her black hair and narrowed her eyes. 'You concentrate on your job,' she said icily. 'I'll concentrate on mine.'

'Oh, don't you worry about me,' said the troubadour, strumming lightly on his lute as he sat himself down on the bed and put his feet up. 'You keep knocking them down, and I'll keep taking the glory.'

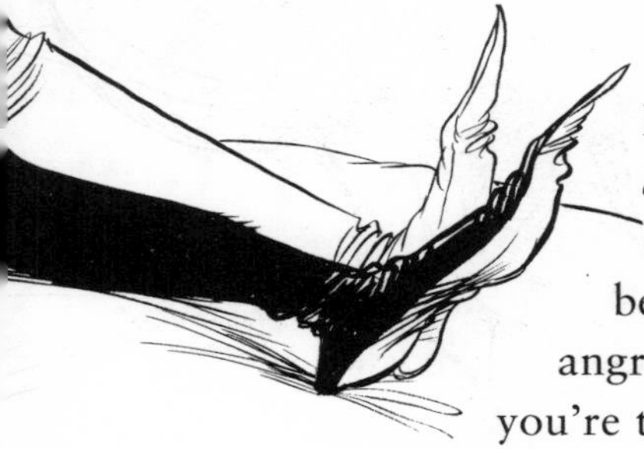

The handmaid's hands flew to her hips. 'If that was *all* you were doing, it would be fine,' she said angrily. 'But I swear you're turning into her ladyship's lapdog. Trailing after her the whole time, tongue hanging out...'

The troubadour threw back his head and laughed. Then, laying his lute aside, he jumped to his feet and went to take the handmaid in his arms.

'Get off me!' she shrieked, and scratched at his face with her sharp, pointed nails.

The troubadour seized her by the wrists before she could do any damage. 'Put away your talons,' he said. 'I'm only play-acting.' He smiled. 'You know I only have eyes for you, my raven-haired sorceress.'

I saw the handmaid visibly soften. 'I can never stay angry with you for long,' she said softly, and shuddered. 'It's this place. The sooner we leave, the better.'

The troubadour nodded. 'It's a great shame that brave Free Lance is not here,' he said thoughtfully. 'It would have made things so much easier.'

'It doesn't matter. I'll take care of the free lance,' she said, hitching up her long gown and hurrying to the door. 'And just make sure you're not too busy "play-acting" to take advantage of it when I do,' she called back.

The troubadour sat himself back down on the bed and started strumming the lute, and singing, in that rich, honeyed voice of his that so thrilled all the ladies.

'My love has eyes of emerald green...'
He paused and chuckled. 'Or should that be,
My love has hair of raven-black...?'

All at once, he stopped playing, jumped to his feet and tucked his lute under his arm. 'Best be off,' he said. 'After all, a banquet isn't a banquet without a troubadour.'

As he left the room, I pulled my boots on at last, buckled up my breast plate and emerged from behind the screen. My shoulder ached, but it was the least of my worries. I didn't know what the troubadour and the handmaid were up to, but it seemed to involve yours truly. One thing was certain, if her ladyship thought she could rely on the troubadour, she was making a big mistake. I hated to be the one to break the bad news, but for the time being at least it could wait.

Right now, I had to get to Wormrick and Jed. In the meantime, her ladyship could enjoy what she thought was her last banquet; the Finalists' Banquet.

Not that you'd catch *me* in that viper's den – not after the day I'd just had. No, I planned to be as mysterious as the Blue Knight. There would be *two* empty seats at the high table that evening.

Using the old tossed-stone trick to distract the guard at the gate, I slipped away from the castle and darted off between the collection of costly tents and elegant marquees. I kept to the shadows, my head down and eyes on the look out for any sign of danger.

Ahead of me, the rocky thistle patch, where the more modest knights like myself had pitched their tents, came into view. I saw at once that something was very wrong.

6

As I approached, I spotted two burly oafs dressed in Duke Wolfhound's colours standing outside my tent, flaming torches in their hands. They were clearly waiting for someone, and it didn't take a genius to work out who.

The larger of the two, a powerfully-built goon with cropped red hair, noticed me. An ugly smile spread across his blotchy face.

'Just the knight we've been looking for,' he sneered and nudged his companion, a pasty-faced oaf with a scar down one cheek.

Scarface smiled. 'That's right,' he agreed. 'You see there's been an unfortunate accident.'

'Accident?' I said.

'Yes, sir knight,' said Scarface. 'A fire.' He lowered

the torch and held it to the tent-flap. With a crackle and a puff of smoke, a sheet of blazing yellow leapt up the side of my tent.

'Tut tut,' said Ginger, drawing a great cudgel from his belt. 'First your tent accidently burns down, and then you have a nasty fall.'

'I do?' I said, my hand gripping the handle of my sword.

'That's right,' said Scarface. 'A very nasty fall. Two broken legs, I believe.'

I drew my sword as Ginger lunged. The heavy cudgel whistled past my ear. He wasn't trying to break my legs – it was a crushed skull he was after.

I stepped to one side and drove the handle of my sword hard into the pit of his stomach. As he lurched forward, I gave him a crushing blow to the back of the head. The great oaf crashed to the ground.

'Sweet dreams,' I muttered.

One down, one to go. I spun round to

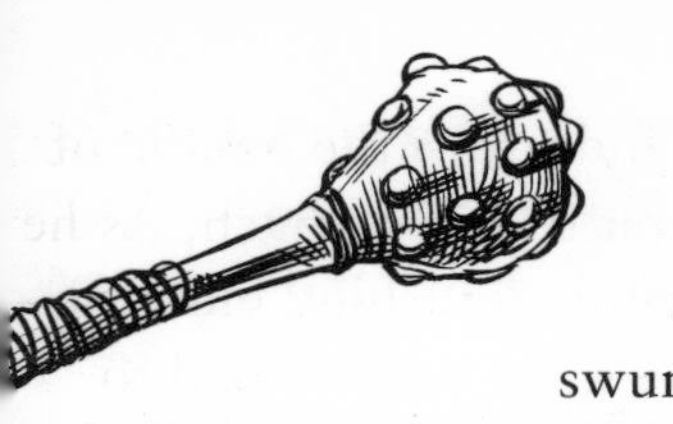

see Scarface, a mace raised above his head, about to brain me. I swung my sword in a low, slashing cut that drew a red line across the blue and white quarters on his chest. It was just a flesh wound, but it did the trick.

Scarface dropped his weapon and let out a long, loud squeal, like a greased runt at a pig-catching contest. I took a step forward. But he'd clearly had enough. Turning on his heels, he fled without a backward glance.

I sheathed my sword and took stock. My tent was now fully ablaze, the fire devouring the tentcloth like a plague of fiery moths.

Suddenly – with a loud *whumpph*! – the whole lot collapsed.

Practically everything I owned had been in that tent, but I didn't care about that. No, what was really on my mind was the fate of Wormrick and Jed.

I dashed off to the stables, praying I'd find them both there, safe and sound. I elbowed my way through the crowd of knights and squires

that had gathered to watch the fire, and burst in through the stable-doors.

'Wormrick!' I bellowed. '*Wormrick*!'

Ahead of me, there came a soft rustle from one of the far stalls, and a spotty face peered up at me from the straw.

'Oh, sir,' he said as he climbed to his feet. 'I've been so worried. The duke sent a couple of his men to find you.'

'I know,' I said, smiling. 'They gave me quite a warm reception.'

'I just grabbed what I could and came here,' Wormrick went on. 'First thing I did was to disguise Jed. That patched surcoat of his is a bit of a give-away. So I swapped it over, hid myself and waited. I didn't know what else to do.'

'You did well, Wormrick,' I said. 'I'm proud of you.'

Just then I felt hot breath on the back of my neck. I turned and saw Jed standing beside me, dressed in a black and silver surcoat. I recognized it at once. It had belonged to the Rich Kid's war horse.

Maybe Jed sensed that he was draped in the surcoat of a dead horse. Maybe the commotion outside had unnerved him. Whatever, he was certainly not his usual self, pawing at the ground, rolling his eyes and gnashing at the bit.

'It's all right, Jed,' I said, patting him on his neck. 'Everything's all right.'

Soon he was snorting down his nose into my face and licking at the saltiness in my palms as if nothing at all had ever been the matter. Outside, the commotion got suddenly louder. Jeers and whistles rose up above loud, angry voices.

'Wait here, Wormrick,' I said. 'I think our friends are back. Guard Jed. And make sure no one touches him.'

I drew my sword a second time, headed for the stable doors and strode outside. A semi-circle of faces greeted me, each one uglier than the last. Ginger and Scarface were among them, and in the middle of the line, Duke Wolfhound himself. As our gaze met, his eyes narrowed menacingly.

'I thought we had a deal, sir knight,' he hissed. He looked round and addressed his henchmen. 'It seems that these days, knights aren't to be trusted – but then what can you expect from a free lance?'

'It takes two to honour a deal,' I replied calmly. 'You didn't mention the war-lance when we made our little agreement,' I said, my shoulder throbbing at the memory.

'Ah, yes, that,' said Duke Wolfhound. 'I'm afraid Hengist got a little over-enthusiastic. He's no longer in my employ. And neither,' he added pointedly, 'are you. Guards!' he bellowed. 'Seize him!'

As one, the burly oafs advanced towards me, their cudgels and maces swinging.

Things weren't looking good. My throbbing shoulder was about to become the least of my worries.

'Stop wight there!' cried an outraged voice.

It was the herald, buttoning up his tabard as he hurried towards us. His eyes fell upon Duke Wolfhound.

'So this is where you've got to, your Gwace,' he said. 'Shouldn't you be at the banquet attending to your guests?'

'Yes, yes,' said the duke. 'I have a small matter to clear up here first, herald,' he said. 'I shan't be long.'

The herald pursed his lips. 'Your Gwace,' he said, 'if you have a pwoblem with one of your knights, it is usual to consult the hewald.'

Duke Wolfhound looked flustered. 'I... I didn't think...' he began.

'That is the twouble,' said the herald sharply. 'You didn't think!' He stepped forward. 'I am the hewald. I weport diwectly to the Gwand Tournament Council. If they were to hear of this, then your status as the host of a gwand tournament might well be at wisk.'

'But... but...' the duke began.

'Never mind your "buts",' said the herald. 'There have been a number of complaints at this tournament alweady. Horses behaving oddly. Stwangely large bets placed on complete outsiders,' he continued, staring pointedly at Duke Wolfhound. 'And it has also come to my notice that a tent has been burned down.'

Shamefaced, Ginger and Scarface looked down at their boots.

'And now I find a knight about to be molested,' he cried. 'I won't have it! Not at a tournament of which I am the hewald! Call off your men, your Gwace, or the next tournament you'll host will be of the village gween vawiety! I twust I make myself clear.'

Duke Wolfhound scowled. 'Yes,' he snarled, and clicked his fingers.

His henchmen backed off, and the whole lot of them slunk away. I turned to the herald. 'Thank you,' I said.

'Don't thank me, Fwee Lance,' he replied sharply. 'Knights like you attwact twouble wherever they go. You don't belong in a major tournament. But since you're here, it is my duty to make sure the wules are followed to the letter!'

With that, he turned on his heels and strode off. I watched him go. A stickler for the rules he might be, but that was exactly the type I needed to make it to the end of the tournament in one piece. After that, however, I'd be on my own.

I went back to the stables. It was warm inside after the chill wind which had got up outside, and the straw smelled sweet and inviting. I slumped down, curled up and closed my eyes... The next thing I knew, Wormrick was shaking me by the shoulders.

'I've rubbed down Jed and polished your armour, sir,' he was saying. 'And her ladyship has sent a tray of quails eggs from the castle kitchens for your breakfast.'

Duke Wolfhound hadn't finished with me yet. I knew I'd need more than quails eggs to see me through the long day ahead.

I had yet to discover just how long that day would be.

7

A trumpet blast echoed round the soggy tournament field. The excited clamour of the crowd died down and all eyes fell on the herald, who strode forward, his boots sinking into the mud with every step. The heavy morning rain had given way to a persistent drizzle and I was wet and cold.

At the far end of the field, I saw the Blue Knight climbing awkwardly into the saddle. Beneath me, Jed trembled.

'What's up boy?' I whispered. Usually the trumpet blast would have him pawing the ground and champing at the bit, but not today. No, today Jed was lethargic, yet nervy, and had hardly touched his breakfast, even though Wormrick had served him up the finest oat-mash the castle had to offer.

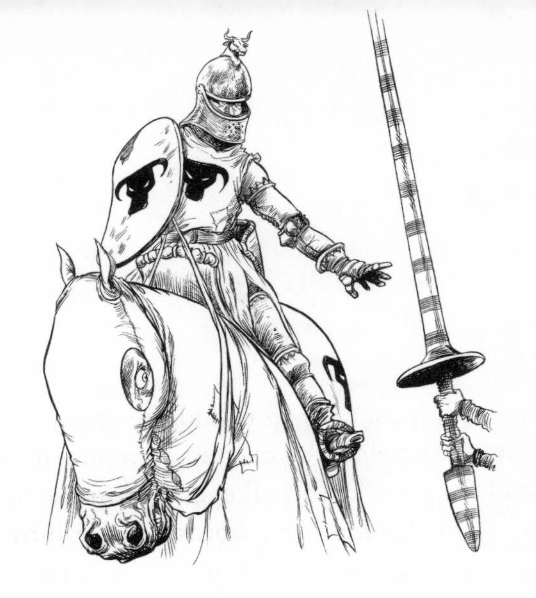

'Everything all right, sir?' came a voice, and I turned to see Wormrick standing beside us, my lance in his hands.

'I'm worried about Jed,' I told him. 'Are you sure none of the duke's men has got to him?'

'They couldn't have, sir. I was with him all evening. I'd have noticed any funny business.' He paused. 'Mind you, there was one thing...'

'Yes?' I said.

'No, it's nothing, sir.'

'Tell me, Wormrick.'

'Well,' he said, his brow furrowing. 'It was that lady.'

'What lady?'

'Her ladyship's handmaid,' he said. 'You know, the one with the black hair.'

'What about her?' I asked.

'It's just that when I first got to the stables, she was there. With Jed. Patting him, she was, and whispering into his ear. She was ever so gentle, though. Said she loved horses, sir, and that Jed was a particularly fine creature,' he added. 'So I didn't see any harm in it, sir.'

'No, Wormrick,' I said. 'I'm sure there wasn't.'

'Look,' said Wormrick, pointing. 'There she is now, sir, staring at Jed. Can't keep her eyes off him.'

I turned, looked up at the raised grandstand – and straight into the poisonous gaze of the raven-haired handmaid. A thin smile danced on her lips.

I shivered. I had a bad feeling about this, a really bad feeling.

In front of her sat her ladyship, next to Duke Wolfhound.

A second trumpet blast echoed round the field, and her ladyship arose. Her face was as white as a sheet and she was trembling violently.

The Blue Knight had taken his lance from his squire, and was holding it like a matron with a walking-stick.

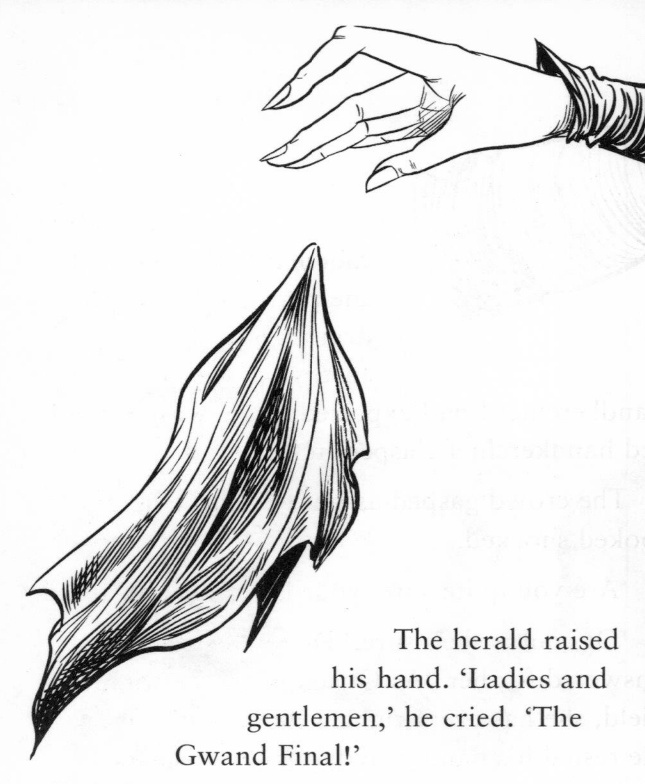

The herald raised his hand. 'Ladies and gentlemen,' he cried. 'The Gwand Final!'

A loud cheer went up. The herald turned towards the grandstand. 'If your ladyship would be so kind.'

Ashen faced, her ladyship fumbled with the silken purse in her hands. Scowling, the duke nudged her roughly, and I saw him raise his hand to conceal the words he hissed at her.

She nodded. The next moment, she dipped into the purse and raised her arm high in the air. Instead of the gold ıandkerchief I had expected, there was a blood ed handkerchief clasped in her hand.

The crowd gasped as one. Even the herald ooked shocked.

'Are you quite sure, your ladyship?' he asked.

'Of course she's sure,' Duke Wolfhound ınswered for her. 'As Queen of the Tournament ield, she has every right, I think you'll find.' Ie rested his hand heavily on her shoulder. Release it,' he snarled.

Tears streaming down her cheeks, her adyship let the handkerchief drop. It fluttered to he ground like a wounded sparrow. The herald tepped forward.

'A field-of-blood joust,' he announced, his oice quavering. 'A fight to the death.'

I shook my head. So this was what Duke Wolfhound had planned. It was clever. Devilishly clever. If the Blue Knight killed me, then the duke would have got his revenge. If, on the other hand, I beat the Blue Knight, I'd have to kill him to claim the champion's prize. Wolfhound clearly didn't think I had the guts to do it, which meant he wouldn't have to pay out. Either way, in his twisted mind, he ended up winning.

Life in the majors! I thought with a shudder. It might look glamorous from the outside, but inside it was rotten.

'Let the field-of-blood joust commence!' the herald cried.

I turned to Wormrick. 'May as well get this over with,' I said. 'Wish me luck!'

The trumpet sounded a third time, and I twitched Jed's reins. He didn't move. From the grandstand, I could feel the raven-haired handmaid's gaze on us, like a hawk eyeing its prey.

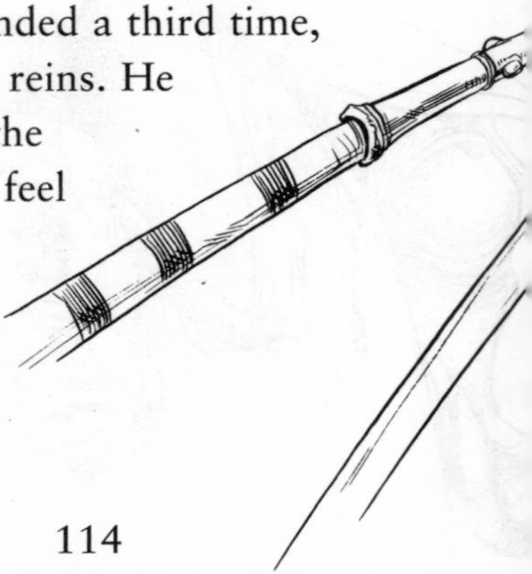

'Come on, Jed,' I urged. 'Don't let me down, ıot now...'

All at once, Jed lurched forward and mmediately picked up speed, galloping over the pongy ground. The Blue Knight hurtled towards me, flapping about like a fat abbot on a donkey, his lance all over the place. I couldn't miss.

I really hated to do this to him, whoever he was – but I had no choice. It was him or me. I lowered my lance into position.

All at once beneath me, I felt a tremendous spasm run through Jed's body from head to tail. Arching his back, he crashed into the sodden field, sending me flying through the air. The ground rushed up to meet me. The next thing I knew, there was a roaring noise in my ears and I was seeing stars.

There was mud everywhere; in my eyes, my mouth. I spat out the foul-tasting filth as I scrambled to my feet.

From behind me, came the pounding of hoofs. I lurched round.

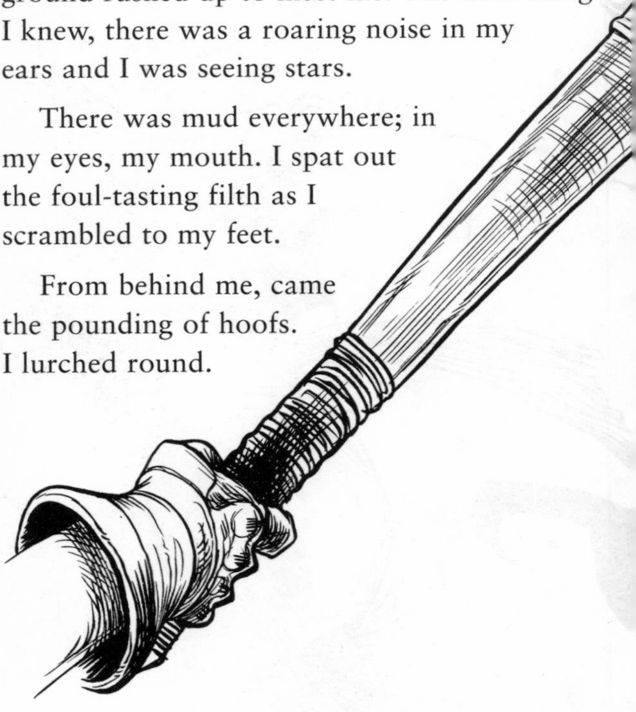

The Blue Knight was bearing down on me, a great studded mace in his hand. Before I could react, the mace struck me and I went down for a second time.

I became aware of the crowd screaming and shouting and baying for blood. I rolled over. The Blue Knight had dismounted. His mace lay discarded behind him. In his hands was a heavy-looking broadsword which hissed through the air as he approached to finish me off.

There was blood in my mouth, the sun in my eyes... I never imagined that it would end like this.

The Blue Knight stood over me and raised his sword above his head, ready to plunge it into my heart. He was so close I could see his blue eyes twinkling from behind his visor. *Too* close...

With every last ounce of strength, I kicked out and took the knight's legs out from under him. It was his turn to come crashing to the ground. I was on my feet in an instant, and on him, my sword at his throat.

The crowd roared with delight.

...to the death. ...to the death – the herald's words echoed inside my head.

Just then, I heard an unspeakable screech from the grandstand. I looked round to see the raven-haired handmaid racing towards me, her talons drawn, her teeth bared and her thick black hair streaming back behind her.

'*No*!' she screamed. '*NO*!'

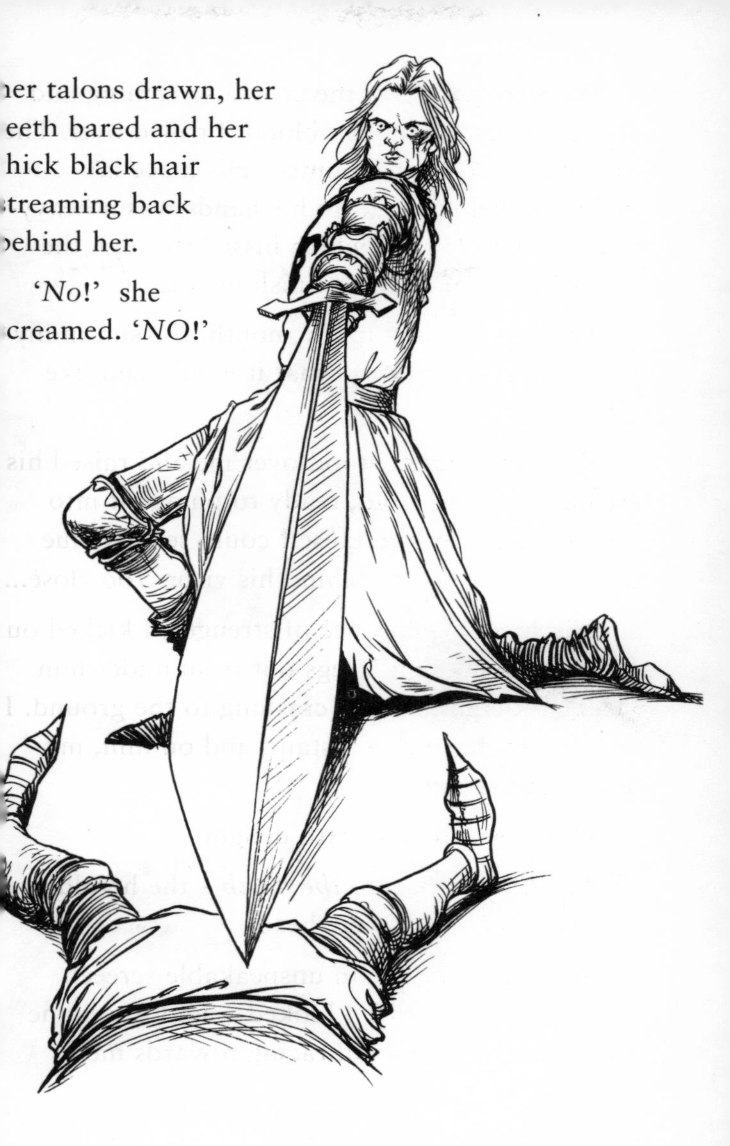

Two men-at-arms leapt forward and pulled her back.

'No! No!' she cried. 'I won't let you kill him!'

A murmur went round the crowd.

I glanced up at Duke Wolfhound. An evil sneer played on his lips. 'It's a field of blood, Free Lance!' he smiled, his fangs glinting. 'You're going to have to kill him if you want your money.'

With a nod, the herald confirmed that the duke was right. 'Wules are wules,' he murmured.

'I won't kill a man without seeing his face,' I said, and drew my sword back. 'Take off your helmet.'

The blue knight did as he was told. And there, staring back at me, was the handsome face of the troubadour.

From the grandstand, her ladyship gave a scream and jumped up from her seat.

'What are you waiting for, sir knight?' the troubadour said bitterly. 'Go on. Finish me off...'

'No! No!' screeched the handmaid, struggling with her captors. 'Don't listen to him, Free Lance. He is no knight, anybody can see that. He's just a poor troubadour. He doesn't deserve to die. It was *I* who bewitched your horse, and all the others, so that he would win the tournament. And then we'd be rich enough to be married and give up this wandering life...'

'Married? But he loves *me* !' her ladyship cried from the grandstand.

'Loves you?' The handmaid glared at her ladyship. 'He could never love a pampered princess like you. You were just a plaything. He told me so.'

Her ladyship stared imploringly at the troubadour. A cruel smile played on his lips.

'It was fun while it lasted,' he said. 'But now it's over. What are you waiting for, Free Lance?'

'You heard the scum,' Duke Wolfhound sneered. 'He's only a troubadour. He won't be missed.' He laughed when I did not move. 'Just as I suspected. Our brave Free Lance here hasn't the stomach for a field of blood. My money's safe!'

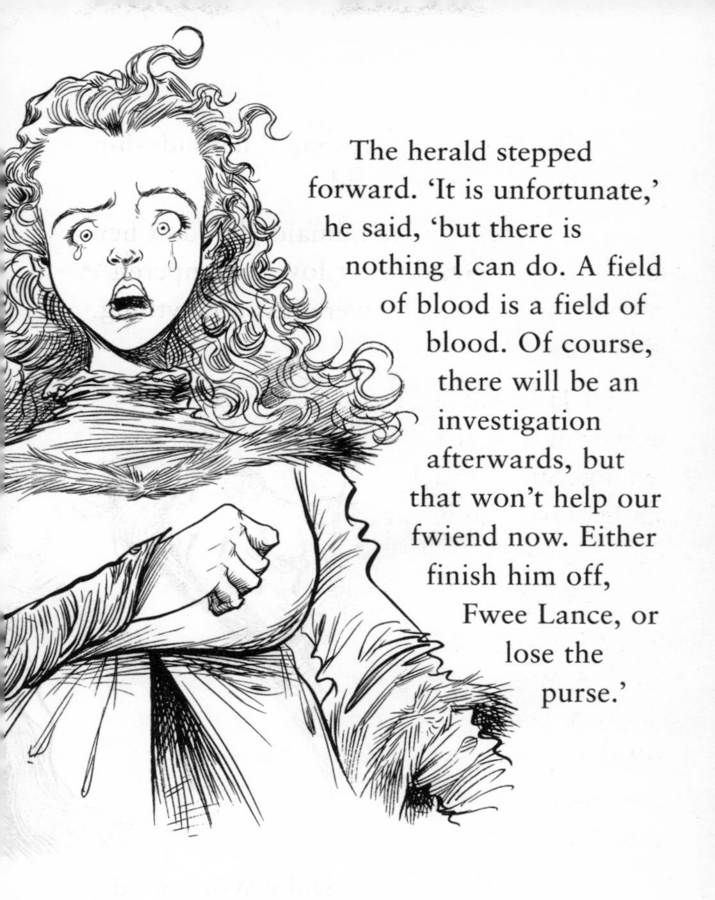

The herald stepped forward. 'It is unfortunate,' he said, 'but there is nothing I can do. A field of blood is a field of blood. Of course, there will be an investigation afterwards, but that won't help our fwiend now. Either finish him off, Fwee Lance, or lose the purse.'

I looked around.

Her ladyship was sobbing, Duke Wolfhand was sneering, the handmaid was wringing her hands. As for the troubadour, he was glaring at me defiantly.

'Kill! Kill!' cried a couple of voices from the crowd, and soon the whole lot of them were chanting loudly. 'Kill! Kill! Kill!'

I raised my sword – and returned it to its sheath.

I looked round at the jeering faces, as the chanting abruptly gave way to catcalls and boos. And at that moment, I knew I'd had it with the Major Tournaments. From now on, I'd stick to the manor-house circuit and the occasional village-green.

'You all disgust me,' I said, spitting on the ground as I turned and walked away from the tournament field.

Jed came trotting up to me as if nothing had happened, with Wormrick running behind him. It was good to see them. I couldn't wait to get away from the place – but first, there was one last thing I had to do.

*

'Thank you, thank you, brave sir knight,' her ladyship said, her emerald eyes sparkling brightly. 'I don't know how I can ever repay you.'

'I'm just glad to have been of help,' I said.

'Oh, you have,' she cried. 'Without you, I would never have got out of the clutches of my wicked uncle.' She looked around. 'And I'm sure I'll be happy here. They're good people.'

I nodded. She was right. They might not be able to joust, but the east country noblemen had kind hearts.

We were standing in front of the manor house of one of her distant cousins, and as she waved goodbye, I knew that I'd be leaving her in good hands. And with the thirty gold pieces Duke Wolfhound had first bribed me with, she'd be able to hire a more reliable handmaid than the last one.

The raven-haired sorceress had been drummed out of town with that troubadour boyfriend of hers. As for Duke Wolfhound, he'd saved the prize money and I'd talked the herald out of reporting him to the Grand Tournament Council. In return, the duke had let her ladyship go. If he was ashamed of making her drop the red handkerchief, he showed no sign of it.

I sighed. I might not have taken the winner's purse, but at least I had no blood on my hands. And besides, one good thing had come out of the whole escapade. A faithful squire.

'Where to now, sir?' he asked as we galloped off.

'I've no idea,' I replied.

'Sir?' said Wormrick, looking confused.

'You are a squire to a free lance now, Wormrick,' I said. 'I can't promise you riches, or soft beds, or warm hearths – but there's one thing I can give you in plenty.'

'What's that?' asked Wormrick, his voice deep and steady.

'Adventure,' I said.

The End

MISS FISCHER'S JEWELS

MISS FISCHER'S JEWELS

Jenny Alexander

Illustrated by

Michael Reid

Hamish Hamilton • London

HAMISH HAMILTON LTD

Published by the Penguin Group
Penguin Books Ltd, 27 Wrights Lane, London W8 5TZ, England
Penguin Books USA Inc., 375 Hudson Street, New York, New York 10014, USA
Penguin Books Australia Ltd, Ringwood, Victoria, Australia
Penguin Books Canada Ltd, 10 Alcorn Avenue, Toronto, Ontario, Canada M4V 3B2
Penguin Books (NZ) Ltd, 182-190 Wairau Road, Auckland 10, New Zealand

Penguin Books Ltd, Registered Offices: Harmondsworth, Middlesex, England

First published 1996
1 3 5 7 9 10 8 6 4 2

Filmset in 15/23 Bembo

Made and printed in Great Britain by Butler & Tanner Ltd, Frome and London

A CIP catalogue record for this book is available from the British Library

ISBN 0-241-13524-9

Contents

Chapter One

The Terrible Day

HANNAH STONE WAS not a girl who liked to show her feelings. If she was angry or upset, she would never throw a tantrum or burst into tears. She left all that sort of thing for her big sister, Beth. One person in the house going off the deep end all the time was more than enough, her parents said – and Hannah agreed. If she had a problem, she would take herself off into a quiet corner, and wait grimly for the bad feelings to pass.

So on the day she had to part with Sherbert, she said not a word, even though her heart was breaking. She groomed him, and saddled him up. She took him out, for the last time, through the woods and up on to Cheriston Moor.

He had been Beth's horse really, given to her by a school friend whose family couldn't keep him any more, because they were moving to the city. Mum and Dad hadn't wanted to let Beth accept him, because they were worried about the cost of keeping him. But Beth had ranted and raged as usual, until she got her own way.

Dad said it wouldn't be long before Beth lost interest in him anyway; they could manage for a couple of months, and then sell him. But it was more like a couple of weeks before Beth decided that having a horse was too much like hard work, so Hannah stepped in to look after him, until they could find a buyer. And Hannah fell in love with him.

For five wonderful weeks, Sherbert had been Hannah's horse. But now a buyer had been found, and Sherbert was going to a different stables. Hannah's parents were relieved, for money was tighter than ever since the new supermarket had opened, and Dad's mobile shop was losing business. And then, to top it all, there was the roof . . .

Hannah came sadly back into the stable yard, and took Sherbert into his stall. She took off his saddle, and rubbed him down. She fed him and then, with a small sigh, she kissed him on the neck and turned away. She stood in the yard drinking hot chocolate with the other girls, until her mother came to collect her.

"Of course," her mother said, as they drove out into the lane, "you can still always come up here for a ride if you feel like it. Mrs Deacon's bound to be able to find you a horse."

Hannah gazed out the window at the fields flashing by, and thought, "I'll never go back there again. How could I?" For if she did, she would always remember Sherbert, and that would be too hard for her to bear.

As they came into the outskirts of Cheriston, Hannah's mother gave up trying to make her feel better, and they finished the journey in silence. Hannah was glad. It was bad enough that they had sold the horse – it would be even worse if they expected her to be cheerful about it.

They turned into Chestnut Grove. Hannah's house was a little bungalow, set well back from the road in its own large garden. It was quite old and tatty, but Hannah had always thought that it was perfectly fine. She looked at it now with a different eye. She saw that house as the cause of her unhappiness. For if it hadn't been needing a new roof, perhaps the family could have afforded to keep Sherbert. As it was, they were already going without crisps at playtime, cakes at tea-time and pocket money, in order to pay off the loan, and there was not a penny left to spare.

For a long time, Hannah stayed in the car. Her mother went indoors to make the tea. She knew that Hannah needed to be alone. For years, she had just been grateful that Hannah never made a fuss like Beth. But now she was beginning to worry about her, in case she was becoming too passive and withdrawn.

Outside in the car, Hannah stared at the house. The bad feelings churned around inside her like dirty clothes in the washing-machine. She didn't want to get them out. If she did, she might say rude and hateful things, and make it worse. She sat there, absolutely still, and nobody who didn't know her well could possibly have guessed how upset she was.

Eventually, she followed her mother into the house. On the floor in the corner of the living room, there was a mixing bowl, underneath the place where the first drips had started coming through the ceiling. It had been there for a while, and was covered with dust. She remembered how, at first, it had seemed like fun, waiting for the rain to come, listening to the drips. Now, she hated that stupid bowl. She would like to smash it in the fireplace. With a sigh, she went through into her bedroom.

Hannah shared a room with Beth. She had never minded that. When they were younger, they had played together all the time. Then, the room had been full of Sindy dolls and Lego houses. Now, Beth was nearly fourteen, and she didn't want to play any more. The Sindys were in a box under Hannah's bed. Beth's bed was like a ship adrift on an ocean of strewn tights and knickers, school books, boxes of talcum powder and used tissues. Eye pencils and pots of blusher were scattered across her bedside table, with bits of cotton-wool, stained pink, or brown, or blue.

All these things that came with Beth's

growing-up, Hannah had found rather glamorous. But she looked at them now with a different eye. They were spoiled, as her whole life was spoiled, by the loss of Sherbert. Now, instead of seeing lots of exciting things that she would grow into one day, Hannah looked at her sister's side of the room, and saw only a horrible mess.

"Hi!" Beth said. She was sitting on her bed, painting her toenails with bright pink nail varnish. "What's up?"

She had forgotten that today was The Day. The Terrible Day. How could she? It just showed how much Beth cared about Sherbert, Hannah thought, bitterly. It just showed how much she cared about anyone!

Hannah walked out of the room. Her feet were heavy, like her heart. She went through the kitchen, and opened the back door. Slobber, the dog, looked up at her, but even he knew when she was in a leave-me-alone mood. She crossed the uneven patio, and strode across the lawn.

The grass was ankle-deep, with daisies and dandelions growing in vigorous clumps all over it. There were trees. The flower-beds had nettles and brambles springing up amongst the bedding plants. It wasn't that no one in the family liked gardening. It was that they all liked the garden to be a little wild. Mr Stone said that Nature was the best gardener you could have. But whereas before it had been like a magical jungle, now, to

Hannah, the garden, like everything else, was only a horrible mess.

In the farthest corner of the garden, there was an old potting-shed. Hannah pushed open the door. Grass and moss grew abundantly on all the shelves. There was a damp and earthy smell. It was a soothing smell. This was the place Hannah always came, when things got bad, like when Beth went berserk over something, and Mum and Dad had a row about how to deal with her. Hannah sat down on the broken concrete floor, and stared into space.

Probably, she would have stayed there until bed-time. But pretty soon she heard a familiar noise from the other side of the wall. Snip. Snip. Miss Fischer was pruning her roses.

"Hannah," she said, softly. "Are you there?"

How did she know?

"Yes," Hannah replied.

"Was it terrible, darlink?"

She hadn't forgotten! Miss Fischer, who forgot everything, had remembered what was happening to Hannah on this day. Hannah was touched. She came out of the potting-shed and climbed on to the wall.

"No, it wasn't too bad," she said.

She dropped down into Miss Fischer's garden, light as a cat. Her face gave nothing away, but inside, she was kicking and screaming and bursting apart, with anger and grief and dismay.

Chapter Two

A Friend in Need

MISS FISCHER WAS wearing a green silk dress that reached almost to the ground. She was old, and rather fat, and her feet, in their tiny black shoes, looked too small to hold her up. Her hair was quite white, except for one broad stripe of black, which swept up across it like the plumage of some exotic bird. She wore lots of pale face powder, and bright red lipstick. Around her neck hung a long string of pearls.

"Did you ride him, darlink, one last time?" she asked.

To hear her speak, you would almost think Miss Fischer was English. She worked very hard at sounding English. The only thing that really gave her away was that hint of a 'k' at the end of 'darling'. However much she tried, she simply couldn't get rid of it.

"I did ride him," Hannah managed to say.

Hannah had known Miss Fischer since she was six years old, when she and Beth used to dare each other to climb over the wall. They were both terrified of her then, of course, with her strange, exotic clothes, and her loud, booming voice. But the first time she caught them in her garden, she wasn't angry with them. She gave them cherries and lemonade, and told them stories about her young days. Perhaps she was lonely, living all on her own. She invited them to call on her again, any time they liked. Beth soon lost interest in her, but Hannah loved going, and they grew very fond of each other. It was a bit like the way things turned out with Sherbert, when you came to think about it. When Beth got bored with the horse, it was Hannah who came to look after him and love him.

"It's nice of you to remember," Hannah said. "Beth didn't."

She couldn't keep the bitterness out of her voice.

"Perhaps she has other things on her mind," Miss Fischer suggested.

"Like painting her toenails?" said Hannah, coldly.

"I expect your poor parents . . ."

"You know what I think?" Hannah interrupted her. "I think my parents should never have agreed to take on a horse, if they couldn't afford to keep it."

Miss Fischer raised her eyebrows.

"If I remember rightly," she said, "they only let Beth have the horse because they didn't expect to have to keep him for long. They weren't to know that you would fall in love with him! And they certainly didn't know that the roof would suddenly need replacing, did they?"

"Well, they should've done," Hannah said, unreasonably.

Miss Fischer sighed.

"I want to tell you something," she said. "Come inside, and we'll have a cool drink."

"You'd better tell me here, if it's important," Hannah suggested. "If we go inside, you'll forget to tell me at all."

Miss Fischer laughed. It was so true! She was incredibly forgetful. How often she had gone all the way to the shops, only to find she had forgotten her purse! Or made a splendid tea, only to remember that she had forgotten to invite anyone. This forgetfulness was one of the reasons why she was so fat – she would often forget she had had her dinner, and have another one! It wasn't that she was silly or vague. The problem was her enormous vitality. She was always so keen to move on to the next thing, that she often forgot to finish the thing she was doing.

She sat down on the garden seat, and patted the space beside her with her hand. Hannah came and sat down, too. She was comfortable with Miss Fischer.

"Many years ago . . ." Miss Fischer began.

Hannah smiled. If anything could take her mind off her problems, it was one of Miss Fischer's stories about her past.

Chapter Three

Miss Fischer's Jewels

MANY YEARS AGO, when Miss Fischer was a girl, she lived with her father in Berlin. The family was Jewish. All their relations, and many of their friends, were Jewish too. They were happy and hard-working. But when Hitler came to power, he began rounding up the Jews and sending them away to camps in distant parts of the country. Miss Fischer's father saw the terrible danger they were in, and before the soldiers came to get them, he took his daughter and fled. They had to leave behind their house, and all the money they had in the bank. But Mr Fischer had a small collection of very valuable jewels, and these he took with him, hidden in his overcoat.

They came to England, and found a place to live. It was easy for Mr Fischer to find work, with so many young men away at the war. They managed to get by. But they lived in a small, damp, rented flat. For Mr Fischer would not sell his jewels in order to buy a house. A house was no good, he said, if you had to run for your life. You needed something you could carry with you. So he kept his jewels in a box under his bed, until the day he died.

"When I was a child, I never had a horse," Miss Fischer told Hannah. "I never had a garden. Or a house. Or anything. Because my father would not spend his money. Well, your parents didn't hide their money away under the bed, and keep it, as we say in England, for a rainy day. If they had, you would never have had a horse at all. And would that really, do you think, have been better for you, darlink?"

Hannah didn't answer. Miss Fischer carried on.

"When your parents have paid off the loan for the roof, perhaps you will have a horse again."

"By that time," said Hannah, glumly, "I'll be growing up, like Beth, and I won't want a horse, and I'll just flop round the house all day being bored, like you have to when you grow up."

Miss Fischer threw back her head and laughed. Her laugh was huge, like a wave, and it swept you up out of your bad temper.

"Come! Some lemonade!" she said, clapping her hands on her knees, and making them wobble.

But when they went indoors, she forgot about the lemonade. She went past the kitchen and straight into the living room. She opened her piano.

"I play for you!" she cried.

Her hands flew across the keys, and the music burst and bubbled out of the piano. Hannah sat in a big armchair, and all the sadness and anger of the whole day bubbled up like the music. She began to cry. The tears came bursting out of her, and the air came rushing in. She felt as if she was suddenly starting to breathe, like a stone statue coming to life. Her body, which had been so stiff and rigid all day, finally started to relax. Miss Fischer kept on playing.

When at last the music stopped, Miss Fischer said to Hannah, "Better now?"

Hannah nodded.

"Tears are like jewels," Miss Fischer

told her. "It is not good to save them up, and hide them all away."

Chapter Four

The Gift

AT THREE O'CLOCK the following afternoon, Miss Fischer put on her apron and rolled up her sleeves. Hannah was coming to tea. At least, that's what she thought. She didn't realize that she had forgotten to invite her.

Afternoon tea, it seemed to Miss Fischer, was a very English affair, and that was why she liked it. She never made *kugglehopf* or *strudel*, things she remembered from her childhood days in Germany. It had to be fruit cake, or muffins, or crumpets – something properly English. Today, she was preparing scones. Miss Fischer's scones were famously terrible, as she usually left them in the oven too long, or forgot to add all the ingredients. But she was convinced that they were really rather good.

It was a great pleasure to be making a special tea for such a special young friend. For Hannah was the only person, now, who really liked to hear Miss Fischer's stories of the olden days. She would listen closely, and then go home and think about it, so that the next time they met, she would have lots of interesting questions to ask. Today, she would want to know, for instance, whether Miss Fischer still had her father's jewels.

Miss Fischer rubbed the fat into the flour. No, on second thoughts, Hannah would know, because she was a bright girl, that she hadn't got the jewels any more. Hadn't she said that it was bad to hoard things? She remembered the diamond tiara she had sold to buy her first piano; the gold necklace that had paid for her training as a music teacher; the pocket watch that had gone on her first smart working clothes; and the wonderful brooch that had provided the down-payment for her house here in Cheriston. She remembered her jewels with gratitude and affection, the same way she remembered her father. But she didn't regret that they were gone.

She poured a little milk into the mixing-bowl, and stirred it in. She tipped the dough out on to the table, and a wisp of flour puffed up. She rolled out the dough, and cut it into rounds, which she laid on the baking tray. She put it in the oven, and switched on the gas. Then she remembered something. The jewels were not all gone! There was one brooch left. She had kept it, just in case. Where on earth had she put it? She picked up the matchbox, and took out a match to light the gas. All of a sudden, it came to her –

the brooch was taped to the back of the painting above the sitting room mantel-piece. Yes! She dropped the matches, and bustled through into the sitting room, to see if her brooch was still there. It was.

Miss Fischer held the brooch in the palm of her hand. It had three large dia-monds in the middle, with smaller stones, mostly rubies, clustered around them. It was amazing how much a little trinket like that could be worth. Enough to buy a horse. Enough for a new roof. Enough for both of those, and some left over. Miss Fischer didn't need it any more. She was old, and there wouldn't be any more rainy days now.

She found a box in the bureau, and dropped the brooch inside. Then she wrapped it in blue paper, and attached a label.

To Hannah – you will know how to use it.
Your friend, Miss Fischer.

As she worked, she was aware of a faint smell of gas, coming from the kitchen. In a minute, she must go and check the cooker. She hid the present down the back of her favourite armchair. She wanted it to be a surprise. Then, she felt such a surge of joy at the thought of making Hannah happy again, that she simply had to have music. She sat down, and opened the piano. Her fingers flew across the keys, and music filled the room. But it wasn't only music that filled the room. Noiselessly, the gas came drifting in through the open door, invisible and deadly.

Miss Fischer closed her eyes. She was drifting on a sea of music. Her head was swimming. She felt dizzy with the pleasure of it. She felt her fingers slowing down. Now, each note hung on the air, waiting for the next one to come. Heaven could not be more beautiful, Miss Fischer thought. And with that, she passed blissfully on to the next thing, in her usual way, leaving her latest plan sadly uncompleted.

Chapter Five
Brave Hannah

AT ABOUT THE time that Miss Fischer was making her scones, Hannah was walking home from school with her sister. She was still cross with Beth for forgetting about The Terrible Day, especially as Beth wasn't sorry at all.

"He was only a horse!" she kept saying.

Hannah couldn't understand why she was being so unkind. She was often thoughtless – but not usually cruel. Hannah just ignored her, and plodded on. She was still sad, whenever she thought about Sherbert. She was glad to have something else to think about – Miss Fischer and her father's jewels. There were a lot of questions she wanted to ask. How many jewels were there? How big were they? What kind of box did he keep them in? She needed all the details, so that she could picture it in her mind's eye, and imagine it all, the way it really was.

As soon as they got home from school, Hannah took Slobber for a walk. He was really her dad's dog. He had bought him to keep him company on his rounds. But Slobber hated going in the van, and Dad had to leave him at home, so it was Hannah who actually looked after him. She felt guilty about ignoring him the previous day. After all, he was as dear to her as Sherbert, and she had had him an awful lot longer. She might have lost one of her special friends, but she still had the other two, didn't she? She still had Slobber and Miss Fischer. She must be grateful for that.

Slobber went eagerly ahead. They could hear Miss Fischer's piano, as they walked down the road. She seemed to be playing something very slow. Hannah had never heard it before. She stopped for a few seconds to listen, but then Slobber disappeared into someone's garden, and she had to run after him and get him out again.

By the time they got home, Miss Fischer had stopped playing the piano. The garden was quiet. Hannah stood for a while by the old potting-shed. There was a light breeze, and she could hear the brown leaves dropping softly to the ground. She climbed over the wall. Miss Fischer's house was closed and silent. She went up to the back door, and knocked. No answer. She peered into the kitchen. There was flour all over the table. Miss Fischer had been cooking something. Scones, perhaps. Was she expecting some-one for tea? Hannah knocked again.

For some reason, she began to feel uneasy. She crossed to the French windows. Now she could see Miss Fischer slumped across the piano. Had she fainted? Had she had a heart attack? With a horrible feeling of dread, Hannah went back to the kitchen door, and turned the handle. She opened the door, and the gas came rushing out. It was overpowering. Hannah took a step backwards, and clapped her hands over her mouth. She felt dizzy, and she thought she might be sick.

Miss Fischer was in the most terrible danger. Hannah took a deep gulp of good fresh air, and then she ran through the gas-filled kitchen, and into Miss Fischer's sitting room, holding her breath all the time. She flung open the French windows, and ran out into the garden again, gasping for air. There was no time to lose. She took another deep breath. Maybe she could pull Miss Fischer out of the house. She ran back inside, with her hand over her mouth. But then she took a proper look at Miss Fischer, lying there across the keys of the piano, and somehow she knew that there was no hurry after all.

"What a splendid girl she is!" thought Miss Fischer's spirit, as she watched Hannah's brave attempts to save her.

She looked down at her own body, and it looked to her like a bag of laundry, propped up on the old piano stool. It was not important, that body. It was no more important than the tin, when you've taken the baked beans out of it. It was something you just threw away. For she felt . . . wonderful! She felt – as indeed, she was – as light as air. She was floating, wafting, flying away towards something new. She was happy that she had given her last precious jewel to Hannah. The child most certainly deserved it.

"Oh, no!" Miss Fischer thought, pulling herself up sharp. "I've done it again!"

She remembered the little box pushed down the back of her favourite chair. No one would ever know it was there. It might be burnt! It might be destroyed! It might be taken off to the rubbish tip! Before she could go anywhere else, she realized, she must make sure that Hannah got her gift.

She couldn't foresee any problems. There was a strong history of haunting in her family. Hardly a night went by in their house in Germany without some dead relative wafting through. Her own dear father had called in for tea at Cheriston once or twice since he passed over. It was a pity she couldn't offer him one of her famous scones any more, but he seemed to cope with his disappointment about that surprisingly well.

She would visit Hannah as soon as possible, and tell her about the brooch. She must do it slowly and gently, in case Hannah was frightened of ghosts. perhaps after supper. It was simply too spooky to go calling on friends in the middle of the night, like ghosts are supposed to do.

Chapter Six
This Haunting Business

HANNAH SPENT THE rest of the afternoon in the old potting-shed, staring at the wall. Everyone knew they must leave her alone. Even Miss Fischer, who was impatient, as ever, to pass on her message, decided she really couldn't intrude on her there.

Hannah's house was empty, except for the dog. Mrs Stone was talking to a policeman in Miss Fischer's front garden, Mr Stone was still at work, and Beth had gone for a walk with her latest boyfriend, Jason. Slobber was lolling around in the kitchen, feeling sorry for himself, because no one was taking any notice of him. Miss Fischer couldn't bear to float around doing nothing until after supper, so she decided to pay him a visit. She could see herself perfectly well – a bit paler than usual, and lot more transparent! – but she didn't know what she looked like to other people, or whether, in fact, they could see her at all. Perhaps you had to learn how to be a ghost. Perhaps it didn't just happen automatically.

She came to Hannah's bedroom window and peered in. It was some years since she had been in there. When Hannah and Beth were younger, she used to babysit for them. But then, one night, she forgot something rather important – she forgot to stay until their parents got home. So that was the end of her babysitting days.

Miss Fischer touched the window pane and her fingers slid through it, as smoothly as they might slide through water. She pushed her arm right in. She was outside, looking at her own arm inside the room. It was extraordinary. She tried to climb up on to the window sill, but her foot fell through the wall. All of a sudden she found herself inside the house, feeling slightly breathless, as if she had jumped into a pool.

On one side of the room was Hannah's bed. Her shelves and beside table. Her wardrobe. All neat and closed up, like Hannah was herself. On the other side, Beth's bed lay partly hidden under a tangle of bedclothes and dirty washing. Miss Fischer was shocked. "Young girls today!" she tutted to herself, as she passed through the door and into the hallway.

There was an oval mirror on the wall above the telephone. Miss Fischer looked into it. To her surprise, there was nothing there. Perhaps a slight mistiness, but that was all. She could hear Slobber at the back door, whining to be let out. It was time for the test. She went in and placed herself right between him and the door. He blinked. Then, with a delighted bark, which said, "Company, at last!", he launched himself at her. The bark changed to a yelp of dismay, as he found himself plunging straight through Miss Fischer, and hitting the back door with a mighty crash. He lay on the doormat, stunned.

Miss Fischer was sorry to have hurt him, but pleased that her little experiment had worked so well. She was obviously visible. This haunting business was a piece of cake! She could hardly wait to get Hannah on her own and have a little chat.

Chapter Seven

A Bit of a Problem

MISS FISCHER'S CHANCE came later in the evening. Hannah was sitting watching television, with Slobber beside her on the settee. Beth was in the kitchen, doing her homework. Their parents were washing up. Miss Fischer popped her head around the open sitting-room door.

"Hello, darlink!" she said, brightly.

Slobber pricked up his ears. Hannah glanced at him and then went back to her programme. Miss Fischer stepped inside.

Now Slobber lifted his head and looked at Miss Fischer. He gave a little whine of pleasure and his tail thumped on the cushions.

"What is it, boy?" Hannah asked, following his gaze. She couldn't see what he was getting so excited about.

"Can't you see me, darlink?" cried Miss Fischer, in dismay.

Slobber stood up on the settee and barked to show Miss Fischer that he certainly could see her, and very pleased he was about it, too! He jumped down from the settee and flung himself joyously at her. But instead of the soft, silky folds of Miss Fischer's dress, it was the cold, hard panels of the wooden door that Slobber found himself crashing into. Again! It slammed shut, and Slobber lay, stunned, on the floor in front of it.

Miss Fischer winced, and said sorry to the dog, before stepping lightly over him to go and sit down beside Hannah. She put her hand on Hannah's arm. It slipped straight through, and came out the other side.

"Oh, bother!" cried Miss Fischer.

But Hannah couldn't see or hear her at all. She jumped up and ran over to Slobber, going straight through Miss Fischer, and making her feel quite peculiar.

"Are you all right, Slobber?" asked Hannah, putting her arms around his neck.

Then she heard her dad outside the door, asking if anything was wrong. He was rattling the handle, but he couldn't get in. Hannah pulled the dog out of the way.

"What's going on?" her father cried.

"It's Slobber," Hannah said, in a puzzled voice. "He just threw himself against the door."

"What did he do that for?" said her mother, coming in with a tea-towel in her hands.

Hannah shrugged.

"Is there something wrong with him, do you think?" she said, anxiously.

Beth said, "The dog's going senile, that's all."

"What's senile?" Hannah asked.

"Old and silly," said Beth, in an offhand way. "Like your other friends."

"Beth!" said her mother, sharply. "How can you be so horrible to Hannah, when she's having such a terrible time?"

Hannah just stared at them both, blankly. Things were getting too much for her. First Sherbert, then Miss Fischer, and now even Slobber . . .

"She doesn't care!" Beth said. "Look at her. Cool as a cucumber! It's me who's suffering, isn't it?"

"What on earth do you mean?" her father demanded.

"No crisps, no sweets, no pocket-money, no babysitting money, no trips, no discos . . . all because of your rotten old roof." She burst into tears.

"*Our* rotten old roof," her mother corrected her. "We all live in this house." She put her arm across Beth's trembling shoulders. "The thing is, Beth . . . you can't make yourself feel better by making someone else feel worse. Can you?"

"Yes, you can!" Beth shouted, shaking herself free. "You jolly well can!"

And she stormed out of the room, in floods of tears.

Miss Fischer stood in the middle of all this, and not one of them knew she was there. Only Slobber, who kept looking up at her, warily.

"His eyes are rolling up!" cried Hannah. "He's going to die!"

"Don't be silly, dear," her mother said. "He's just upset. Like all of us are. Why don't we put on his favourite video? Come on."

They sat down on the settee, Hannah, her mother and the dog. Hannah's father sat in one of the armchairs. Miss Fischer sat in the other.

"Oh, dear," she thought.

Perhaps this haunting business was actually going to be a bit of a problem after all.

Chapter Eight

Hannah Gets a Cold, and Miss Fischer Has an Idea.

IN THE MIDDLE of the night, Miss Fischer stood by Hannah's bed. If ghosts walk at night, like they're supposed to do, she thought, then perhaps that's because they show up more in the dark. After all, ghosts are generally believed to be white, and she was certainly looking paler than usual. Perhaps she would glow in the dark!

She gave a little cough. Hannah didn't stir. She said Hannah's name. Still, Hannah didn't stir. She took a deep breath and shouted at the top of her voice. But her huge, loud scream came out tiny and small, like the faraway moan of the wind. She stamped on the floor; she jumped up and down. If things go bump in the night, she thought, then how on earth do they do it? It was very vexing. She sat down on the bed. Hannah shivered, and pulled her quilt more tightly around her.

Now, here was an interesting thing.

Could it be that she made the air around her cold? Miss Fischer got up, and crossed to Beth's bed. She leaned over her. Beth nestled down more deeply in her untidy heap of bedclothes, like a little hedgehog in its winter pile of leaves. So, if they couldn't see her, and couldn't hear her, at least they could feel that she was there. She would stay close to Hannah in the morning. Hannah was bound to wonder what was making her chilly. She might think something odd was going on. She might be on the look-out, then, for any little signs Miss Fischer might be able to think up.

It didn't quite work out that way. Hannah shivered so much at the breakfast table, that her mother decided she must have caught a chill. She was sent off to bed with a hot-water bottle and a warm, milky drink. If Hannah thought anything odd was lurking around, she assumed it was an unfriendly germ, and never dreamt that it might be a friendly ghost.

Mrs Stone went to work as usual, but promised to come home as early as she could. She gave Hannah her work number and told her to ring if she had any problems.

"Slobber will look after you," she said. "Are you warm enough?"

Hannah nodded. She was much warmer. But then, Miss Fischer had retreated to the far side of the room and was leaning against the window sill, watching. She would have Hannah and

Slobber to herself for the whole morning. Surely there must be something she could do to make Hannah notice her.

She reached across and touched one of the blusher pots on Beth's bedside table. She tried to push it. Her fingers went straight through. Something smaller then. She tried a scrap of cotton wool. It was no good. There was a heap of talcum powder on the carpet. She crouched down on all fours, and gave a big blow. She pushed with her fingers. Even the tiny grains of powder were solid and immovable to her touch. It was quite depressing. What now? Miss Fischer sat down on Beth's bed, and rested her chin on her hand.

Hannah lay in bed, staring at the ceiling. Slobber kept an eye on Miss Fischer, but he didn't try to jump up any more. He had learnt his lesson about that! Then suddenly Hannah turned her head, and looked straight at Miss Fischer. But she didn't see her. She saw Beth's bed.

Hannah got up and put on her dressing-gown. She went up to Beth's bed. Miss Fischer moved away. Hannah began to push all the dirty clothes and scraps of tissue, and last week's homework, and spilt talcum powder, underneath her sister's bed.

"It's not that I'm cross with her . . ." she told Slobber, as she worked.

Although, of course, she was.

"It's not that I don't like her any more . . ." she said.

Although, of course, she didn't.

She opened the drawer of Beth's bedside cabinet, and swept all the bits of used cotton wool, and the open tubes of face make-up, and the broken eye-pencils into it.

"It's just that I need some space. I need everything to be smooth and clear."

The dog watched her, attentively. He seemed to understand.

"I want to tidy away all the clutter, Slobber. I need to clear away all the bad stuff. I want to have nothing left of it. See?"

She looked around the room. All the surfaces were empty. She pulled the covers straight on Beth's bed. She was satisfied. Now the room was all her own.

"I feel better now," she said to Slobber, fondling his floppy ears. "Stronger."

She thought he understood.

Miss Fischer understood. It occurred to her that she, too, might feel stronger in her own environment. Perhaps that was why ghosts usually appeared in the houses they had lived in, and not on motorways, or in swimming pools, or in other people's homes. If she could somehow get Hannah to come to her house . . .

Hannah lay down on her bed again. She was very tired. Slobber jumped up beside her. He was a big dog, and there was only just room for him.

"Thank goodness I've still got you," she told him. "I just don't know how I could get through all this without you."

She closed her eyes, and very soon she began to doze.

In Miss Fischer's mind, an idea was forming. It was, perhaps, a desperate measure. But pretty soon they would be selling off her furniture. When time was of the essence, then surely desperate measures were called for.

Chapter Nine

So Far So Good

HANNAH WAS SOUND asleep. Slobber lay beside her, with his chin resting on her tummy, looking at Miss Fischer with a quizzical eye. They were old friends, him and Miss Fischer. For it wasn't only Hannah who liked to call on the old lady when times were hard. If he was bored, or lonely, or in disgrace, he would wriggle through the gap at the far end of the garden wall, and she would give him bone-shaped biscuits from his special jar and stroke his head. Now here she was, all of a sudden, in his house. Perhaps times were hard for her. He wanted to make her feel welcome. But, on the other hand, he didn't want to keep smacking into things.

"Hello, darlink," Miss Fischer said to him, softly. He pricked up his ears.

"Would you like a bone biscuit?" she went on.

He sat up on the bed. Hannah rolled over and sighed, in her sleep.

"You come with Miss Fischer," Miss

Fischer said.

Slobber jumped down off the bed.

Miss Fischer was about to take the direct route through the closed window, but she stopped herself just in time, before Slobber had a chance to come crashing through after her. The bedroom door was ajar. She stood back to let him go first. He could pull it open; she couldn't. The kitchen window was open. It was an escape route Slobber often used. They went to the bottom of the garden, and through the gap. Miss Fischer was pleased with herself for remembering he couldn't just slip through things like she could. But then she forgot, and filtered straight through her own back door. Slobber tried to follow her. Bang!

He stood, dazed, on the doormat, shaking his head.

"Sorry darlink," Miss Fischer called, from behind the door. "You wait. I shall open the door."

It was easier said than done. She did feel stronger in her own house. She could move a cobweb with her finger, and in the kitchen mirror, she could clearly see herself – faint and transparent maybe, but more than the wisp of mist she had seen when she looked in the mirror in Hannah's house. If Hannah could be persuaded to come here, Miss Fischer felt certain she would be able to see her. And surely she would search everywhere for Slobber. She needed him. Hadn't she said so? She knew he liked to hang around in

Miss Fischer's house. She was bound to come.

Miss Fischer picked up the back door key; at least she could manage something light like that here. She put it in the lock. But she couldn't get it to turn. Her fingers just kept slipping through it. She could hear Slobber outside, whining to get in. He wasn't the most patient of dogs. She didn't want him to give up on her and go wandering off home.

Well! If she couldn't let him in to get a biscuit, she must take the biscuits out to him. She tried to pick up the jar, but it was too heavy. She managed to pull it slowly across the worktop. It teetered on the edge, and she put her hands underneath to catch it. It toppled over into her hands, dropped straight through them, and smashed into a hundred pieces on the kitchen floor.

Outside the door, Slobber went berserk. He could hear his biscuits, he could smell his biscuits . . . and he wanted to eat his biscuits!

"One moment, darlink!" cried Miss Fischer, snatching up a handful of broken biscuits and making for the door. She slid through it like a knife through butter, but the biscuits, being real and solid, did not. They thudded against the wood, and dropped down on to the doormat, and however hard poor Slobber pressed his nose into the gap under the door, he couldn't even get a nibble of them.

He began to dribble. He was a champion dribbler! They hadn't called him 'Slobber' for nothing!

"Never mind," said Miss Fischer, sitting down on the step beside him. "Soon, Hannah will come, and she will be able to see me here, and I will tell her, 'Get poor Slobber a biscuit!' How does that sound?"

It sounded unconvincing. By the time Hannah came, Miss Fischer would have forgotten all about his biscuits!

Slobber sighed, and looked gloomily up at her.

Miss Fischer gave him a little smile. She was relieved to see that he didn't seem to be going anywhere. So far, so good, she thought.

Chapter Ten

Time Is Running Out

SOME TIME LATER Hannah woke up and found Slobber gone. She didn't get up and go looking for him. It was the last straw. It was more than she could bear. She wanted to cry. At first, she tried to stop herself, by staring hard at the blank walls, and the empty surfaces of the room. But then she remembered what Miss Fischer had said about tears. And she lay in her bed, and let the tears come streaming down her face.

The first one home was Beth. She glanced into the bedroom and saw her bed all smoothed out, and her precious things all gone, and she was furious. She stormed in to have it out with Hannah, but stopped dead when she saw her. She had never in her life seen her sister cry. It shocked her. She had always been such a tough little thing. Beth sat down on the bed, and put her hand on Hannah's arm. She felt guilty about all the horrible things she had said. She felt sorry.

"Where's the Slob?" she asked, gently.

"He's gone!" Hannah sobbed.

"He'll be back," Beth said.

But Hannah just went on crying.

Meanwhile, Miss Fischer was sitting patiently in her garden with Slobber, waiting for Hannah to come. She tried to make Slobber bark. But he didn't feel like barking, and you could never make him do anything he didn't want to do. Eventually, Miss Fischer went and looked in Hannah's window to see if she was awake yet. She saw the two girls on Hannah's bed, crying on each other's shoulders. She was horrified. What had she done? She called to Slobber. She would have to find some other way of making Hannah come to her house.

Miss Fischer led Slobber right back

into Hannah's room. On her way out again, she noticed the local paper, lying on the doormat. The back page was all notices of auction sales. There was a picture of Miss Fischer's house. *Sale of House and Contents*, it said underneath. *Date, Tuesday, 9th October. Viewing, Monday 2-5pm.*

She had only one week left, before some stranger would come and buy her old armchair, and take away with him Hannah's wonderful gift! Time was running out!

Chapter Eleven
The Viewing

THE WEEK FLEW past. Miss Fischer tried everything she could think of to make Hannah notice her. She jumped up and down on the television, making the picture go wobbly. She blew as hard as she could on the radio, making the sound go fuzzy. She turned hot drinks cold, by putting her hands around the cup, and she took the warmth out of the fire by standing in front of it. But it was no good. The sole result of all her efforts was that Mr Stone decided the house was awfully draughty, and stuck strips of sellotape round all the doors and windows.

Monday morning came, and Miss Fischer thought her only chance was to play for time. If she could frighten the people who came to the viewing, then they wouldn't want to come back and buy anything. So when the agent put his sign up outside her door – *Sale here tomorrow. Viewing now on* – and opened up the house, Miss Fischer was ready and waiting.

People kept coming all through the afternoon. Men in suits, and men in dungarees. Women in hats, and in jeans. Little children, who fingered the lace chair-covers and the tasselled curtains. Babies who dribbled on the carpets.

Miss Fischer flitted between the rooms, in what she hoped was a ghostly way. But the only ones who seemed to notice her comings and goings were the children. The babies chuckled. The toddlers pointed and giggled. An older boy, who was off school with a tummy ache, actually struck up a conversation with her. His mother, seeing him apparently chatting to a dining-room chair, thought he must be getting a fever, and wanted to take him home. But his father just said,

"Leave him alone. It's just a pretend game, isn't it? You know what kids are like!" And he went back to examining Miss Fischer's crystal chandelier. Miss Fischer jumped up on to a chair and pushed the crystals with her hand. They swayed slightly. There was a faint jingling sound. The man took a step back, and eyed it suspiciously. The boy laughed.

If the grown-ups couldn't see her, Miss Fischer thought, she would just have to start to mingle with them a bit. She made them shiver as she passed among them. She touched the piano keys and people turned their heads and frowned. She fluttered the pages of sheet music. She rustled the leaves of her prize aspidistra.

Everybody who came to her house

that day left it uneasy, or even alarmed. There was something spooky about it. They didn't want anything from that eerie house. Who would buy a piano that tinkled like that, all on its own? Who would buy a pot-plant that stirred and rustled, even when there wasn't any breeze? And who would want to stand through hours of bidding, in a house that made their flesh creep?

But there was one person at the viewing who was completely unaware of these ghostly goings-on. It was Mrs Stone. And she was unaware of Miss Fischer's antics for the simple reason that Miss Fischer kept well away from her. If Mrs Stone was planning to come to the sale the next day, there was always a chance that she might decide to bid for the old armchair. It was a very small chance. But, by now, Miss Fischer was clutching at straws.

Mrs Stone wasn't looking for furniture. Her house was full to bursting already. What she was looking for was some small memento of Miss Fischer – something for Hannah to remember her by. There were ornaments and bowls on the mantelpiece. Perhaps one of those would do. A pair of porcelain dogs in the fireplace. An old-fashioned table lamp. She wandered across to the piano. There were lots of things on it, crammed together, ready for the sale.

Among them, she found the very thing. It was a small wooden box, with a metal clasp. Hannah would like that. She had boxes of every shape and size stacked away in her cupboard. She kept all her bits and pieces in them. She needed them, because she hated to leave things lying around.

"Seen anything you fancy?" the agent asked Mrs Stone, as she was leaving.

"Just one thing," she replied. "A little box . . ."

Miss Fischer groaned. There was nothing more she could do. It was out of her hands now. But it was not in her nature to be gloomy for very long. She would stay around for the sale, and if some stranger bought the chair, she would move on. On to the next thing. That had always been her way.

Chapter Twelve

Miss Fischer's Moment of Triumph

THE NEXT DAY, being Tuesday, Hannah should have gone to school. But when her mother told her about the little wooden box, she got very excited, and said she simply had to see it. It could be

The Box – the one Miss Fischer's father had hidden his jewels in, when he had brought his family out of Germany. She remembered the last time she had seen Miss Fischer, and all the questions she had wanted to ask. Now she would never know what had happened to the jewels, or whether Miss Fischer had any of them left. But if she could see the box and hold it, perhaps she would somehow get a sense of what had happened.

So Hannah and her mother went early to the sale, arriving there before anyone else, and having time for a good look around. Hannah felt strange, being back in the house now that Miss Fischer was gone. She stood silently in the sitting room as the people began to arrive. There weren't many people. The auctioneer said he couldn't understand why it was such a poor turn-out.

Miss Fischer's table linen and her best tea set were the first things to go. They weren't particularly familiar to Hannah. She watched with interest as the sale went on, and things she had never seen before came under the hammer. And then the auctioneer got to the ornaments on the piano. Hannah looked at the piano and the empty piano stool. She remembered all the times Miss Fischer had played for her, and she missed her. The feeling was so strong and sudden, it made her catch her breath. It was like a real pain. She longed to see Miss Fischer . . .

And then – she could see her! Sitting

on the piano stool, looking exactly the same as ever. Well, except that she was transparent, of course.

"Miss Fischer!" Hannah gasped.

"What, dear?" said Mrs Stone.

"Miss Fischer – loved that piano," Hannah said, staring at the old lady.

"Darlink!" said Miss Fischer, delightedly. "I've been trying to get through to you for days!"

The auctioneer tapped his hammer, and moved on to the next item. It was the little box.

"Do you think that box might have belonged to Miss Fischer's father?" Hannah whispered to her mother, hoping that Miss Fischer would give her the answer.

"Maybe . . ." her mother said.

"No," said Miss Fischer. "Now, listen, darlink. I have something important to tell you . . ."

Hannah said, softly, "What was that one like – the one he kept the jewels in?"

The auctioneer said, "Two pounds here . . . two pounds fifty, the lady in the corner . . . you, madam, three pounds . . ."

Hannah's mother was too busy bidding for the box to notice Hannah any more.

"I said, I have something important to tell you," Miss Fischer repeated. "So don't change the subject or I might forget what it was!"

Hannah grinned. Miss Fischer said, "You must buy the chair. You know – my favourite armchair. I wish you to have it."

This didn't seem to Hannah to be such a very important message. What on earth did she want a moth-eaten old chair for? Weren't there much more exciting things to talk about, under the circumstances?

"What's it like being dead?" Hannah asked.

"I don't know, dear," said her mother, who had managed to outbid everyone else, and was now the proud owner of Miss Fischer's little box.

". . . and now we come," said the auctioneer, "to this fine old armchair. Who will start the bidding? Who will give me three pounds?'

Hannah put up her hand.

"Good girl!" cried Miss Fischer, who

had jumped up on to the table in excitement.

"Hannah!" said Mrs Stone. "What on earth are you doing?"

"I want the chair," said Hannah.

"But we haven't got room for it," her mother objected.

"Three pounds fifty, you sir . . ." said the auctioneer. "And am I bid four pounds?"

Hannah raised her hand again.

"I've got that lovely little box for you, Hannah," Mrs Stone reminded her. "Surely you don't need an ugly great chair as well?"

"Four pounds fifty, the man in blue . . . five pounds, anyone?"

Hannah raised her hand.

"Yes, yes!" cried Miss Fischer, tap dancing on air.

She was still as fat, and still as lively, but lighter now, and her tiny feet no longer looked too small to hold her up.

"Five pounds. Five pounds for the chair . . ." The auctioneer scanned the crowd. "Five pounds fifty, anyone? No? Then it's five pounds once, five pounds twice . . . five pounds, to the little girl in green!"

"Yes! Yes! Yes!" yelled Miss Fischer, joyfully.

She had done it! The chair was safe! She knew that Hannah would never part with it. It, and everything in it, was hers. Hers, forever.

"Got to fly, darlink!" cried Miss

Fischer, impatient as ever to be moving on.

And, with that, she shot up into the air and disappeared through the ceiling, leaving Hannah staring after her, open-mouthed.

"Oh, bother!" Miss Fischer thought, as she went sailing up. "I remembered to tell her to buy the chair, but I forgot to tell her why!"

But it was too late now. She simply couldn't bear to hang around any longer!

Chapter Thirteen

Beth Makes a Discovery

HANNAH PUT THE chair in her bedroom, and sat down on it. She wondered why Miss Fischer had wanted her to have it so much. It seemed an odd choice. Why not the jar she had kept Slobber's bone biscuits in? Why not the mugs they had drunk hot chocolate from so many times?

"Why did you want me to have this chair in particular?" she asked softly.

But nobody answered. Miss Fischer had gone.

Hannah sat in her chair, and it was curiously comforting. She was glad she had bought it. She loved it already. Not that she expected Beth to love it, too. It really did clutter up the bedroom.

"I'm sorry, Beth," she said, when her sister came home from school. "I know it takes up a lot of room. But I wanted it so much . . ."

"No problem!" said Beth, flopping down on her bed. "There's going to be pots of room around here from now on, because I've decided to keep my things tidy!"

Hannah was speechless with surprise.

"No, really," Beth went on. "I've been a pig! But it never occurred to me you minded about my mess. You never said anything about it, did you? But then, you never say anything about anything. You don't have tempers and tantrums like the rest of us do, so sometimes it seems as if nothing matters to you."

Hannah stared at her in astonishment.

"That's why I got fed up with you, actually," added Beth. "I mean, I was suffering, and I didn't really see why you shouldn't suffer too."

"What do you mean?" asked Hannah.

"Well . . . when we got our pocket

money stopped because of the rotten old roof, and I threw a wobbler, you just . . . you just accepted it. And that made me feel even worse."

"It doesn't mean I wasn't angry too."

"I know that now. But then you didn't even get stressed about Sherbert, and I thought you just didn't have any feelings at all. I mean, if I'd loved that horse as much as you did, I'd have hit the roof about them wanting to sell him! I wouldn't just have let them! So you going quietly off to the potting-shed just made me feel like . . . well . . . like some sort of frantic freak."

"Sorry," Hannah said. "I had no idea."

"Me neither," said Beth, giving her a smile.

"What're we going to do then?" asked Hannah. "It's no good expecting me to have tantrums and stuff – I just can't!"

"I know. But you could say how you feel, couldn't you?"

Hannah nodded.

"And I could try to listen!" said Beth. "That's not easy for me, you know!" She stood up. "But first I'm going to do something else that's not easy for me . . ."

Hannah watched her sister take off her school uniform, and hang it in the wardrobe. Yes! She hung it in the wardrobe! She watched her take some clothes from the heap on the floor, picking off the bits of used tissue, and the little balls of hair she had cleaned from her brush some days before. Then came the big spring clean.

Beth put the lids on all her bottles and tubes, and lined them up neatly on the shelf above her bed. She folded some of the clothes on the floor and put them in her drawer. She took her prized collection of dirty underwear and put it in the washing machine. She ventured into the dark regions under the bed, where old toffees lurked, all covered in dust. She retrieved a fossilized doughnut. She even brought in her age-old enemy, the vacuum cleaner.

By tea-time the bedroom was transformed. Hannah, who thought this was what she had always wanted, was oddly disappointed. She was touched that Beth had wanted to please her but now the room was too clean, too clear, and Hannah missed the chaos and disorder that was so much part of Beth. After a few days, she was starting to plant things on Beth's side of the room – a dirty sock here – an open tube of make-up there – as if the whole heap might grow again from that. But Beth always tidied these little seeds of messiness away.

Before Christmas, the builders came and mended the roof. The weather was dry and cold. To Hannah's relief, Beth was beginning to slip back into her old ways. A discreet scattering of knickers and tissues could be seen on the bedroom floor, like a light covering of snow. The make-up came down from the shelf. Beth had another new boyfriend, and she couldn't concentrate on anything else. It was love! Her side of the bedroom erupted once again.

So it was that, on the night of the Year Ten Christmas disco, Beth was frantically searching among her things for her Iced Blackberry lipstick. She burrowed and rummaged, scattering debris behind her, like Slobber scattering earth from the flowerbeds on one of his bone hunts.

"Have you had it, Hannah?" she demanded, desperately.

"Of course not," Hannah said.

"Can I look in your things?"

"Be my guest."

Beth searched Hannah's drawers and shelves. She slid her hand down the back of Hannah's chair.

"There's something here!" she cried.

She brought out Miss Fischer's little surprise. She read the label.

"It's a present from Miss Fischer! She must've forgotten to give it to you!"

Hannah tore the blue paper off it, with trembling fingers. Beth called their mother.

"What's up?" she said, appearing in the doorway.

Hannah stood by the window, holding the brooch in the palm of her hand. The three big diamonds sparkled in the yellow December sun. They were so bright, they made her eyes water.

"It's nice . . ." Beth said. "A bit old-fashioned, of course . . ."

"It's a token of Miss Fischer's affection," said their mother. "That's what counts."

"It's more than that," Hannah told them both. "I think it may be worth a lot of money."

She told them the story of Miss Fischer's flight from Germany, with her father and his jewels. They listened patiently.

"Hannah, dear," her mother said at last, "I'm afraid that's all just an old lady's romantic notions . . . She was a bit confused, you know, towards the end. They can't be real diamonds. Nobody has diamonds as big as that."

"But it was a lovely story," Beth added.

Then she started her search again. She

never found the Iced Blackberry. She had to settle for the Crushed Strawberry, in the end.

Chapter Fourteeen

The Three Diamonds

EARLY THE NEXT morning, Hannah pinned the brooch to her jacket and set off to catch the bus. Her plan was to look in all the jewellers' shops in Cheriston High Street, and see what a brooch like hers would cost to buy. She didn't believe for one moment that Miss Fischer was confused. And she didn't think she was a fraud, either. In which case, the brooch simply couldn't be a fake, could it?

But there was nothing similar in any of the jewellers' shops' windows. She would have to go into one and ask. The man in Perryman's looked the most approachable, so that was where she went.

"Do you . . . value things?" she asked him.

"Yes," he said. "But we have to make a charge, of course."

Hannah was crestfallen.

"I haven't got any money," she told him.

She had spent her savings on Miss Fischer's chair, and she hadn't had any pocket-money since the roof began to leak.

"What is it that you want valued?" the man said, kindly, taking pity on her. "Perhaps I could just have a little look at it."

She took off the brooch. The man put on his spectacles, and clipped a magnifying glass over one of the lenses. He examined the brooch for a few seconds, and then he let out a long, low whistle.

*

When Hannah told her parents how much the brooch was worth, they were astounded.

"What are you going to do with it?" her mother asked.

"Sell it," said her father, immediately,

"and put the money in the bank, I should say."

But Hannah shook her head. She thought she knew what Miss Fischer would have wanted her to do with it. The same thing she must have done herself, all those years before, when she became the owner of her father's jewels.

"I'm going to break it up," she said. "One of these diamonds will buy me a horse, and his stabling fees for life. That's something I really want. One of them will pay off the bank loan for the roof, so we'll be able to have treats and pocket-money again. That's something we really need."

"Hear, hear!" Beth agreed heartily.

"What about the last one?" said her mum.

"The last one I'm going to put in that little box you got me at Miss Fischer's auction sale, and keep it under the bed."

"Under the bed?" exclaimed her father. "What's wrong with the bank?"

"In an emergency," Hannah told him, "you can't always get to the bank, can you? You need something small, that you can carry with you."

"But, Hannah . . ."

Hannah wasn't listening any more. She looked at the three diamonds. Soon, there would be only one left. But the other two would not be lost. They would simply be exchanged, one for a horse, and the other for the new roof. Not so long ago, she had had three special friends. Now there was only one left. But the other two were not lost. Nothing was ever lost. Their love, and all the things they taught her, would be part of her life forever.